THE IMPOSSIBLE CURE

"What is it, Lois?" Demi asked, her hand on her heart. Her legs felt like they were turning into jelly. She really believed she was about to faint.

"It's Jodi."

"Oh, God."

She felt the tears coming.

"No...she's...completely better," Lois said.

"What?" Demi shook her head as if her ears weren't working correctly. "What are you saying, Lois?"

"Jodi. She went into a remission so quickly and so completely, the doctor's stupefied."

"I don't understand."

"No one does. They've tested her twice. They can't find any evidence of cancer. You should see her. She's eating everything in sight, and she wants to go home. Demi, it's a miracle!"

ANDREW NEIDERMAN

THE MAGIC BULLET

LEISURE BOOKS NEW YORK CITY

For George and Annie, my parents,
who gave me the foundation upon which to build my castle.

And for my wife, Diane,
who is and always has been my Magic Bullet.

A LEISURE BOOK®

December 2008

Dorchester Publishing Co., Inc.
200 Madison Avenue
New York, NY 10016

ISBN 10: 0-8439-6189-9
ISBN 13: 978-0-8439-6189-8

The name "Leisure Books" and the stylized "L" with design are trademarks of Dorchester Publishing Co., Inc.

Printed in the United States of America.

10 9 8 7 6 5 4 3 2 1

Visit us on the web at www.dorchesterpub.com.

THE MAGIC BULLET

PROLOGUE

Eight-year-old Jodi Walker lay terminally ill in the Palm Springs Desert Hospital. She was in a private room and resembled a doll in the large hospital bed. Strands of her once vibrant golden-brown hair looked more like fading hay brushed over the pillow. Her hazel-green eyes were almost always closed now, the lids occasionally fluttering spasmodically as if she were struggling to open them. Lying beside her, her favorite doll had its own eyes closed. It seemed to be mimicking her.

No one stated it outright, but whenever visitors for other patients or even hospital personnel looked in on her, a gray pallor came over their faces, and they averted their gaze quickly to deny the morbid reality. It was as if Death had moved closer and closer, its shadow just a moment or two behind, but deep enough and large enough to drape itself over everyone and everything within ten feet of the room.

And whenever Lois and Ralph Walker walked through the corridors, those who knew who they were and what they were about to lose avoided them or looked through them. No face is more filled with pain than the face of a parent about to lose a child. They wore translucent masks of denial, under which were layers and layers of raw horror. One could almost hear the primal anger and pain echoing down the hallways. It reached deep into the very core of those within what now looked to be caves housing the lost and soon forgotten. Visitors tightened their grips on the hands of their ill friends and relatives when Lois and Ralph Walker passed by their doorways, their two bodies moving in a funeral gait, looking detached from their very souls.

As silently as ghosts themselves, the Walkers entered their daughter's room as if they feared they might wake the sleeping patient and the Grim Reaper folded at Jodi's feet. Ralph went to sit at his daughter's side. Lois quietly went to the phone.

Demi Petersen had been expecting her sister Lois's phone call. She had already discussed the subject with her son, Taylor. The Walkers were having difficulty finding blood donors. Jodi's blood type was Type O/Rh negative, and so was Taylor's. Normally, it was preferred that the donor be at least seventeen years old. Taylor was only fifteen, but with Demi's consent, the Walker's oncologist, Dr. Weber, was willing to have him be a donor.

"She needs the platelets," Lois said in a voice that sounded as if it were coming from the bottom of a deep tunnel instead of a telephone. "But Doctor Weber also wants to transfuse white cells. She's not reacting to the antibiotics. I wouldn't ask if we had another choice. You know that, Demi. I hate asking."

"Of course you should ask, and you don't have to hate doing it, Lois. Taylor wants to donate. You know how fond he is of Jodi. He always looked after her like an older brother. They were so cute together," Demi said and stopped when she realized she was starting to couch her words in the past tense.

"I know it's traumatic for a boy Taylor's age to be brought to the hospital and hooked up to tubes that take his blood. It's still traumatic for me, and I'm in my thirties," Lois said and followed it with a slight, thin laugh.

"Taylor won't be upset. You know how he is. He feeds on a challenge, and he loves to confront his fears. He's just like Buddy that way. If you merely imply he can't do it, he'll want to do it more, and he'll do it better than you ever expected. I don't think there's another boy his age who can deal so maturely with his emotions."

Demi could hear Lois's deep breathing. She had to keep talking. If she stopped, she would burst into tears, and especially now, Lois needed her to be strong.

"I look to him for advice half the time. Warren says he's a sixty-year-old man in a fifteen-year-old's body. Although, he usually doesn't mean it as a compliment."

"Are they getting along any better?" Lois asked, not really wanting to hear about it.

"There's an uneasy truce. I guess I should have checked it out with him before I started dating Warren, but it's been nearly two years since Buddy died and . . ."

"Eventually he'll understand," Lois said.

"Oh, Taylor understands. He just doesn't like it. But

that's not important now. What's important is getting him over to the hospital to give the blood. It's wonderful that he is able to do it. When do you need him there?"

"Yesterday. She's bad, Demi. They're not saying it, but I know it's only a matter of days. If we're lucky," she added, and laughed again. "Imagine thinking *that* would make us lucky."

"Stop," Demi said. She was the original ostrich who had faith that if you ignored something enough, it would simply disappear. Their mother always accused her of being unrealistic or burying her head in the sand. "Don't dare say such a thing. I won't hear it. I won't."

"Seems hard to believe, doesn't it? For us, it's still just a bad dream. Both of us keep hoping we'll wake up and laugh with relief. Imagine? I wonder if I'll ever laugh again."

Demi could hear how her sister's throat tightened when she spoke. The words were being squeezed out a syllable at a time as if the Grim Reaper had a tight grip on her neck as well. It wasn't difficult to imagine her grief and depression afterward leading her to the same dark hole.

"Lois, I'm so worried about you."

"Don't worry." The tone of her voice changed to a firmer, almost stoically official one. "I may look like the walking dead, but I'm okay. Bring him in the morning before school, if you can. It's all arranged. Call me if there's a problem and I'll look for other donors. I know how Taylor feels after being at this hospital, the hospital where his father died. You've told me often how he avoids looking at the building whenever you drive by."

"There won't be a problem," Demi promised.

"You know what I was thinking yesterday, Demi? I was thinking how good it is that Mommy and Daddy are gone and they don't have to see this."

This time Demi couldn't speak. She had thought the same thing often. She took a deep breath and squeezed back the tears.

"Lois, you've got to hold yourself together. Somehow . . ." she managed before her own throat tightened.

"I'll call you, if there's any change," her sister offered. It was the best she could do.

After Demi hung up the receiver, she sat on the stool in her kitchen and stared blankly at the microwave as if the glass door were a television screen. Indeed, she was seeing pictures: pictures of Jodi and Taylor, pictures of her and Buddy and Taylor enjoying a Sunday barbecue at Lois and Ralph's house during happier days when everyone she loved was still alive and healthy.

She sighed deeply and ran her right hand through her thick, dark-brown hair, brushing it back and down to her shoulders. Kiki was upset with her for continuing to keep it that long. He never hesitated to say whatever he thought, the consequences be damned. He wanted all of his beauticians to have their hair cut and styled as models for the customers. It was even his self-anointed brilliant idea to have each of his stylists wear a different style so the customers would immediately see choices.

"If all the women in Palm Springs let their hair grow as long as yours, Demi, we wouldn't have much business.

You're setting some example, thank you," he told her, twisting and turning his shoulders so emphatically she thought he would tear himself apart.

However, she knew he was right when it came to promoting his salon, but Demi had resisted because Taylor liked her hair longer, and she felt guilty about her relationship with Warren, guilty enough to want to do things to please Taylor. Warren didn't mind her hair long and didn't care if she cut it short. Any other woman would probably find her lover's indifference troublesome, but she didn't give it much thought. In the back of her mind, even though Warren had moved in, she couldn't see the relationship ever lasting. For now they had fun together, and that seemed to be enough.

"What is it?" Taylor asked. "What's wrong, Mom?"

From the expression on his face, she knew he had been standing there staring at her for a while. He stood in the doorway with his arms folded across his chest, just the way Buddy used to whenever he was getting ready for a serious conversation. Her son was growing more and more like her dead husband. He had Buddy's lighter brown hair and Buddy's deep set, dark-brown eyes. He was going to be tall like Buddy, and slim, too. He had Buddy's smile, which was just a tiny tucking of the corners of his mouth, and a twinkle in his eyes.

And, like Buddy, he always sensed when something was bothering her. He was also just as successful at making her laugh, making her forget. He was the antidote to doom and gloom, the sunshine on a dark cloudy day. Her sister Lois, she thought, would be losing this precious gift, her child. Her own fear of such a loss convinced her that her sister would not survive.

"It was Aunt Lois," Demi said.

"Jodi needs my blood?"

She nodded. "The platelets like we discussed, and also your white blood cells."

"When?"

"Tomorrow morning. We'll go early, before school. Is that all right?"

"I'll have to move the president back an hour or so, but it will be all right," he said.

Demi smiled. "It's very nice of you to do this for your little cousin, honey."

Taylor shrugged.

"What am I doing? If I could invent a cure for leukemia, I would be doing something. What's for dinner?"

"Warren's bringing Chinese."

"He always brings the hot and spicy stuff I hate. Can't you make me some eggs?"

"Is that all you want?"

He thought a moment.

"I read someplace that when a person gives blood he should eat steak. We got any?"

"I think I do have a T-bone in the freezer. I bought it for Warren last week, but he forgot." She looked and nodded. "I'll defrost it in the microwave."

"Warren told me real men eat their meat raw. He said he likes it still wiggling on the plate and then wiggling in his mouth and stomach. I think it even wiggles when he goes to the bathroom."

"Stop," Demi said.

"I'm not joking. He said he likes it biting back."

"Oh, he did not."

"I like it dead," Taylor added.

"I know how you like your steak, Taylor," Demi said. She smiled at him and nodded. "I gave you a good haircut. It's growing in even this time."

Taylor shrugged again. It was really just a quick lift of his shoulders that was so Buddy-like it made her heart ache.

"I didn't think mine was so bad last time. Warren's looked bad."

"No, it didn't," Demi said laughing.

Taylor widened his eyes as if a brilliant thought had just arrived.

"Maybe it doesn't matter what he looks like. Maybe nothing will help."

"Taylor!"

"I gotta go do my homework. Test tomorrow in English. I have to transfuse my knowledge to the paper, too."

"Okay. I'll call you. It's nice what you're doing, honey. Other boys your age . . ."

"I hope it helps," he said and dropped his shoulders just the way Buddy used to when a dark thought crossed his mind. Then he turned and walked off, leaving Demi feeling like she was on a sailboat in a dead calm.

Demi thought there was something magical about the mornings in Palm Springs, especially during March and April. The dark shadows of evening thinned with the sun peering over the San Andreas Mountains and became extensions of dreams, weblike, ethereal, no longer silhouettes cast by the grand brown hills but veils being softly pulled back to reveal the glistening sidewalks and streets, the bright bougainvillea and oleander bushes, the trimmed hedges and lawns along the well-manicured golf courses. It was truly as if some deific magician edged back his grand handkerchief to illustrate his wonder. Where was that magician now, when they needed him so badly?

After Buddy's untimely death, Demi had lost her faith in spiritual things. A heart attack was, ironically, the least feared danger in her mind when it came to him. He should have been the cancer victim, not poor little Jodi. There had been good reason to believe that might happen to Buddy.

A year before Taylor was born, Buddy had been one of a dozen or so people accidentally exposed to a high dosage of radioactivity at the nuclear energy facility in Palo Alto. Many of his coworkers had come down with some form of cancer over the following ten years, but he had no signs of any tumors or blood trouble. They thought he had escaped serious illness. Soured on working in the plant, Buddy became a computer programmer and took a job in Palm Springs. Life was promising again, but two weeks after Taylor's tenth birthday, Buddy had a heart attack on the job. It was truly as if he had been shot.

One day they were laughing and talking about selling their house and building a home in the Indian Canyons of Palm Springs, and the next day she received a phone call telling her he was on his way to the ER. She dropped everything. She had just started dinner. Taylor came with her, and all the time she drove to the hospital, she chanted, "He'll be all right. This is a mistake. It can't be. He'll be all right."

She remembered laughing in the midst of her grief that day.

"Buddy and I were always expecting him to develop some form of cancer. After Palo Alto, the odds were not in his favor. We never thought about a heart attack," she told the emergency room doctor. He listened politely, but he didn't understand because he didn't know about Palo Alto.

For a while afterward, she convinced herself he wasn't really dead; he was just away on a job. In his place, some surrogate volunteered to fake his death.

It was just her way of avoiding reality again, she thought, pretending it never happened. Actually, her sister Lois had it wrong. It wasn't Taylor who freaked at the sight of the hospital because of Buddy's death; it was her. She was the one who had to swallow hard, close her eyes, take deep breaths and then move forward talking about other things, other places. Taylor, as usual, dug his hands into his pockets, put his head down and charged forward.

Maybe that determination stemmed from his short, but caustic conversation the night before at dinner when Demi told Warren that Lois had asked for Taylor to donate his blood.

"Won't do any good," he had said as he chewed and savored the Szechwan shrimp dish. "Just prolongs the inevitable, tortures the kid."

"Warren, how could you say that?" Demi asked. Sometimes he could be so cold she wondered how he could also be so loving. Or was that just simply sexual excitement? Lately, she had been closing her eyes, pretending she was with Buddy. She was afraid Warren would somehow realize it.

"It's easy for him to say it," Taylor remarked. "He's not the one with leukemia."

The way Taylor spoke, it was clear even to Demi that he wished Warren was the one in the hospital. Warren put his fork down and sat back.

"Hear that? Hear the way he talks to an adult?"

"Adult?" Taylor said looking up. He turned his head to search the room.

"Smart-ass. When I was his age, I didn't say a word at the dinner table."

"Probably couldn't think of anything to say," Taylor quipped.

"Taylor. Stop it," Demi said. Somewhere inside, she was laughing, though she kept it well hidden. Warren eyed her suspiciously, searching her lips for the slightest sign of a smile.

"Let me take a hand to him and he'll mind."

"I told you a million times, Warren. I don't believe in hitting."

"Easy to see the result of that," he said, nodding toward Taylor.

"He happens to be an A+ student. All his teachers rave about him."

"They don't have to live with him."

"You don't either," Taylor shot back.

"Taylor, please," Demi said and raised her eyebrows.

Taylor pressed his lips together and then concentrated on his food.

"Kid's right about something," Warren remarked after a few more moments. "I don't."

Everyone ate in silence. Afterward, Warren went out, and Demi went up to Taylor's room. He was already in front of his computer, tapping away at the keys, weaving that magical electronic loom, just the way Buddy used to do it. She watched from the doorway for a while, intrigued and amazed at the child who had come from her body. Surely some of the seeds of this intellectual curiosity had to have been in her, which could mean she never achieved what she was capable of achieving herself. She should have gone to college, perhaps. She had decent grades in high school, and she loved to read.

"Taylor," she said softly. He hit a key and then turned.

"Hi, Mom."

"Don't you think you will ever get along with him?"

"Who?"

"You know who."

"Whom, but who's checking? If you mean that Neanderthal who sleeps in your room and burps like a sick motorcycle every morning when he wakes up . . ."

"He doesn't burp every morning," she said laughing.

"You mean that's you I hear through the wall?"

"What else do you hear through that wall, Taylor?" she asked quickly, her eyes small.

"Nothing," he said and turned back to the computer. "Nothing worth hearing," he muttered under his breath.

"You better get to bed early. We have to get up early to go to the hospital."

"I'll be up before you," he said and she knew he would.

Warren came home late and didn't get up early because he was between jobs. A contractor's life was erratic to say the least. Sometimes he worked for months, six days a week, and then he wouldn't have anything for months. Warren was somewhat more ambitious than most construction workers she knew, however. He liked having money in his pocket and driving a good, late-model automobile. He was a sharp dresser, too, and always up on the styles. When they went out, he liked to splurge, take her to the fanciest restaurants and order the most expensive meals and wines. He had rich tastes and had educated himself when it came to the finer things. Actually, that was what impressed her about him and what made her believe that eventually Taylor and he would get along. That and his terrific body.

The man was carved of stone. His stomach was flat and hard, and when she reached around and grabbed those buttocks, it actually sent a second surge of excitement through her body, driving her to another series of orgasms. She also liked the way Warren made love. It was obviously part of his ego trip to be sure the woman was satisfied. He wanted to hear her cry for mercy. Sometimes she did moan for real, but most of the time, she moaned to make him happy.

After breakfast, Demi and Taylor drove to the hospital. They entered and were directed to the hematology department. Taylor walked in like a trouper, and when the nurse asked him if he had ever given blood before, he shrugged and said, "Sure. There's a vampire living next door."

That set the scene.

"Actually, he's never done it," Demi said. "But I bet he knows all about it," she added proudly.

When the donation was completed, they gave him some juice and had him rest for a while. He was up and eager to go sooner than they expected, however. Demi drove him to school and then kissed him good-bye.

"You did a wonderful thing today, Taylor. I'm very proud of you."

Taylor smiled and brushed back his shock of hair. He started away and then turned back.

"Hey, Mom."

"What now, Taylor?" she said, preparing herself to hear him say something sad about Jodi.

"I wasn't kidding back there."

"What do you mean? Kidding about what?"

"We do have a vampire living next door," he said. "But Warren doesn't have to worry. They feed on human blood only."

"Taylor, stop."

He walked off. When he was gone, she laughed and drove off to work.

And that was how it started. A simple act of human compassion and charity, a gift of giving that helped everyone feel a little better about a horrible thing.

Some time after four in the afternoon the following day, just after Demi had started on her last customer of the day, Kiki called her to the phone, a look of annoyance in his face.

"If it wasn't your sister, I would tell her to call back," he said. "I don't like it when my customers are interrupted. Everyone's time is important. We don't want our customers thinking we don't respect them."

"Give me a break. I don't get many personal calls here, Kiki. You know that, and you know what's happening in my family," she said, wanting to add, "you damn dandy." But she didn't.

Her hand was trembling as she took the receiver. It was going to be bad news. She knew it. She expected it. But that never made it any easier. She took a deep breath, whispered her mother's name and said, "Lois?"

"Demi." She was crying so hard, it was hard to hear her. "Demi."

"What is it, Lois?" she asked, her hand on her heart, which felt like it would pound its way out of her chest. Her legs felt like they were turning into jelly. She really believed she was about to faint.

"It's Jodi."

"Oh, God."

She felt the tears coming.

ANDREW NEIDERMAN

"No . . . she's . . . completely better," Lois said.

"What?" Demi shook her head as if her ears weren't working correctly. "What are you saying, Lois?"

"Jodi. She went into a remission so quickly and so completely, the doctor is stupefied."

"I don't understand."

"No one does. They've tested her twice. They can't find any evidence of the cancer. You should see her. She's eating everything in sight, and she wants to go home. Demi, it's a miracle!"

CHAPTER ONE

Allan Parker had chosen to specialize in oncology like a man bent on vengeance. Just at the start of his second year of medical school, his father called him to tell him his mother had been diagnosed with a malignant breast tumor. A radical mastectomy was performed, but the cancer cells had traveled to her pancreas and liver. It was only a matter of months.

Allan's mother never saw him receive his diploma, nor was she there to celebrate when he was offered a position at the U.S.C. Medical Center. He interned and began to study under Dr. Thornton Carver, a world-renowned oncologist and surgeon, and quickly became his most promising prodigy. No young doctor had ever shown Carver more dedication, more determination. Allan's intensity not only impressed Dr. Carver, it actually frightened him a bit. He wasn't sure whether Allan Parker was an overachiever or simply a man obsessed.

Although Allan stood a little over six feet tall, maintained a trim figure, and was strikingly handsome in a mature way; even though he was only in his late twenties, he had few romantic involvements with women during the period he studied under Thornton Carver. Carver was convinced Allan wasn't gay; it was more like he was asexual most of the time. If, during one of those rare occasions, he did date and start to become involved with someone, he always seemed to have a built-in shutoff valve that caused him to abruptly end the relationship.

Once, when they discussed it briefly over coffee, Allan confessed he didn't want anything or anyone distracting him. A relationship, especially a marriage and a family, would certainly do just that.

"A wife, children, require and deserve at least half your energy and attention. I'm not willing to commit to that right now."

"Well, I would humbly suggest I'm a fairly successful doctor and have a family, Allan," Thornton told him.

"I respect that, Doctor Carver. It's just not for me at the moment."

If anyone else had told him to his face that his life wasn't enough for them, Thornton Carver would have taken offense, but he was continually intrigued by his prodigy. He sat back, smiling, and softly asked, "What do you expect to accomplish, Allan?"

"I expect to find a cure for cancer," he replied nonchalantly, as if the answer couldn't be more obvious. It had the sound of a juvenile's dream, but there was nothing in Allan's face that suggested it was a fantasy. He was damn serious. "I expect to discover the magic bullet."

He was indeed spending every spare waking hour either reading about other cancer researchers or doing his own research.

"Everything tells us that this just isn't going to be one bullet, Allan. You know that some cancers act completely different from others, that some patients who contract lung cancer or colon cancer, melanomas, sarcomas react differently," Dr. Carver said.

"There's a common·thread to it all, some starting point, something that initiates the uncontrolled growth and spread of abnormal cells."

"Well, yes, but . . ."

"The Wake Forest work with cancer-resistant mice strongly suggests the possibility that we are all constantly getting cancer, one cell at a time, but our immune systems detect and kill them."

"I understand that, Allan, however . . ."

"If we can just pin down why and understand our own immune system much better, we could unlock the box that contains the secrets we need," Allan insisted. "Even you have concluded that unexpected spontaneous remissions aren't simply explained away by claiming incorrect diagnoses."

Carver nodded. Who knows, he thought, maybe this young man will make a significant discovery someday. He was certainly relentless. He lived alone in a modest Los Angeles apartment, choosing the location and the apartment simply on the basis of its proximity to work. His friends, if you could categorize them as such, were only people he met at work and people with whom he could discuss or share his labor. Most of them eventually backed away because he simply exhausted them. No matter what the movie or play was that they saw together, he found a way to bring their work into it. If they went to dinner, he talked about the significance of food, the research on nutrition. The same result followed attendance at a concert, the discussion of a new novel, even a walk in the park. Something always led him back to his topic, his work.

"You remind me of Captain Ahab in *Moby Dick*," Gloria Alford told him over cocktails one night. The twenty-four-year-old woman in accounting had dated him twice before, each time waiting for him to ease up and enjoy what they were doing together, to truly enjoy each other.

"Oh? How so?" he asked.

"A white whale bit off his leg and gave him his only reason to live: revenge."

He nodded. She meant it as a negative, but he just saw it as an objective, true observation. It turned out to be their last date—a mutual conclusion.

Oddly enough, even though Allan was a man fully concentrating on the science and devoted to the research, he was not a doctor with a poor bedside manner. He truly empathized with his patients, especially older women. They felt and believed he was in this with them, that their battle was his personal battle. They swore by him; they had faith in him.

"You've got to focus all your mental energies and power on this cancer," he told them, "and think of it as the enemy within. Nothing else should involve your attention. Chant slogans of hate. Will it dead. Hate it!" he advised, with such enthusiasm that they worked to please him more than to please themselves.

After his internship, he had remained at U.S.C. Medical Center as an associate of Dr. Carver's, but whenever Allan lost a patient, he took it far too personally for Thornton Carver, who chastised him continually.

"It's good to give your patients the sense that you care about them, that you see them as people and not as objects, but if you mourn every one of them, you'll burn yourself out, Allan. It will eventually affect your work," Carver advised.

There wasn't a man Allan respected more than Dr. Carver, but this was one bit of wisdom Allan refused to accept.

"When I mourn them, I grow stronger," he replied. Carver nodded. Incredibly enough, there was evidence of that. During the days following the loss of one of his patients, Allan was always at it longer, harder. One of Carver's interns nicknamed Allan "Doctor Sisyphus," and the name caught on. Sisyphus was the mythological king of Corinth whom Zeus punished for disrespect. He was condemned to push a boulder up the side of a pit eternally. It always rolled back down the hill before he could get it out, but he never gave up trying. After a while, his punishment, his tragedy, became his sole purpose for living. Was that true for Allan Parker as well?

Eventually, Allan did hang onto one friend, Joe Weber, another one of the young physicians who studied under Thornton Carver. Joe was a five-foot-seven, stout, dark-haired, but blue-eyed man who was somewhat in awe of Allan. He admired him for his dedication and wondered if he was lacking in that area himself, for, unlike Allan, he was very interested in women and good times and could easily put the work aside and party all weekend.

However, Joe was an excellent student and a fine physician. Thornton was proud of him and strongly recommended him when the Desert Cancer Group in Palm Springs interviewed him for a position. They hired him; he met the daughter of a patient the following year, and four months later, got married. Eleven months afterward, they had their first child and bought their first house. Joe was living about as normal a life as an oncologist could in an age when cancer, in one form or another, appeared to be the plague of the century.

Meanwhile back in Los Angeles, Allan, now in his mid-thirties, remained unmarried, unattached Doctor Sisyphus. He maintained his good looks and trim figure and was at the top of everyone's "Most Eligible Bachelors" list. New interns assumed he was some sort of genius who had already been practicing far longer than anyone else his age. He was odd, but a genius. They saw that he spent as much time in research as he did in the practice of medicine. It seemed he never slept. Was he human?

Despite other romantic opportunities, Allan Parker continued to ride alone, a medical bounty hunter in pursuit of the world's most detested, abhorrent villain. He never shied away from a confrontation with the disease. He moved through the rows of terminally ill like a battlefront medic, angry at his inability to stop the dying, furious at a world that would permit it to go on, raging at the enemy, and remaining more determined, more willing to sacrifice, waiting for his precious magic bullet to reveal itself.

So when Joe Weber called him late in the morning one day to report on an unexplainable, spontaneous remission of a child suffering with leukemia, Allan resembled someone who thought he had been chosen to hear a divine revelation.

"She was diagnosed with acute myeloblastic leukemia nine months ago. She went into remission but relapsed only a month afterward."

"You did a bone marrow transplant?" Allan asked.

"Yes. Ineffective. During the past month or so, I was trying to keep her comfortable, stop the bleeding and infections with platelet transfusions. The condition degenerated. Frankly, I was looking at a few weeks at the most."

"Uh-huh," Allan said, gritting his teeth and clenching and unclenching his fist. He had just lost a leukemia patient who was only in his mid-thirties. He had been diagnosed with chronic myeloid leukemia. Present statistics showed that there were only about two new cases of it diagnosed per 100,000 people in the United States each year, and he had one of the cases. To him it seemed as if the monster taunted him, brought his most cherished victims to Allan's doorstep.

"Two days ago, the girl's cousin donated platelets. I wanted to try some white blood cells to fight her infections as well. She wasn't responding to the antibiotic protocols," Joe continued. "I transfused them immediately that morning. I thought I detected some improvement in her, so I ran the tests immediately. Her white cell count was way up of course, but the numbers made no sense. It was almost as if . . . they cloned themselves. I couldn't make heads or tails of the result. The next day, by two o'clock, her white and red cells were normal, as were her platelets. But here's the big news, Allan. There was no evidence of blasts in her bone marrow. Not a single immature white blood cell. She was full of energy, had an appetite, and looked like she could get right off the bed and walk out. I don't know how to explain this."

"You transferred white cells, too?" Allan asked to be sure he heard it all correctly.

"Yes. I've concluded all other therapies, Allan. I lost all hope of prolonging this child's life. The leukemia was raging."

Allan sat up.

"And now she's in complete remission?"

"A healthier, happier little girl you've never seen. Appetite, energy. I feel like a fool keeping her in the hospital. You believe in miracles?"

"Not in the religious sense," Allan replied. "How old is the girl's cousin?"

"Fifteen. We were raking the area for donors and finally decided to include him with his parental permission. Everyone's nervous about blood transfusions these days as it is, but his blood is O/Rh negative, close as they come to a universal donor."

"You know that there have been some isolated cases of spontaneous remission with this type of cancer," Allan said.

"Yeah, but none of the cases I've read about were this

far along. I'm talking days away from the Grim Reaper," Joe said, lowered his voice, and added, "maybe even hours."

Joe's obvious amazement impressed him. He had come to hate false promises and leads that led to nowhere, however, and practiced a healthy skepticism.

"Can you get the boy in again, get a sample of his blood?"

"I suppose. Do you really think it was the cause?"

"From what you're telling me, it's the most logical place to look," Allan said.

"What am I going to look for?" Joe asked. "Do you know about something new?"

Allan considered and looked at his schedule. "I'll take a ride out there. I want to examine the girl, so don't release her."

"That might be hard considering her condition at the moment, but okay. And?"

"And then we'll see," Allan said cryptically. He checked his watch. "I'll be there as soon as I can. Get at least twenty cc's from the boy," he said.

"Great. You'll stay with us. Toby's always asking why you never come down, and you'll be surprised at how the girls have grown."

"Thanks," Allan said.

After they hung up, Joe thought a moment. He and Allan spoke periodically, but he wasn't kidding about Toby's comment. Up until now, he couldn't get Allan out to Palm Springs, even for a weekend. Actually, what bothered him the most was that Allan rarely asked about his family. He didn't just now either, and Allan had been his best man!

What he didn't tell Allan was that Toby couldn't imagine why he and Allan had even remained acquaintances, much less friends.

"Let's just say I get beside him once in a while and push that boulder up the side of the pit," he replied when she asked him about it once.

"What? What pit? Never mind. Doctors," she said disdainfully and walked away.

Frankie Vico had just hit the big Five-O a little less than three months ago. He knew he drank a little too much and he had smoked too much, but as the half-century mark loomed over him, he began to make significant cutbacks and pay attention to his doctor's prescription to improve his chances for a healthy final trimester on the planet. He left the bowling alley and restaurant like clockwork at 2:15 P.M. and worked out with his personal trainer at his home. He had already made some strides improving his blood pressure, and just by cutting down on booze and eliminating chunks of bread at every meal, he had lost nearly twelve pounds off his 190-pound, five-foot-ten-inch frame the first month. He had his chef, Eddie, buy a variety of low-fat food products and even put some of the diet dishes on the regular menu at the restaurant, not caring if customers wanted them or not.

The restaurant made a small profit, even as other restaurants in Palm Springs and the immediate area went bankrupt during the economic recession, but it was only a front for his cocaine distribution. He was part of Danny Vico's organization emanating from Chicago. It was practically a franchise operation. Danny's father was Frankie's father's first cousin, and of course, despite the satirical way the movies treated it, crime families really did exist and really did care about each other. Blood was blood.

Frankie's customers were all high rollers. Many were snow birds who got his address and made contact before leaving the north or the east for the spectacular desert winters and spring. Frankie was sure the CIA didn't check an applicant any closer. He was proud of how tightly he ran his part of the operation, and he knew Danny was very satisfied with him as well.

"You're not greedy, Frankie," Danny told him last time he had come to Palm Springs. "That's good. You won't make the big mistake."

Frankie knew Danny wasn't referring to a drug bust. Many of Danny's associates were busted and walking the streets soon afterward; he was referring to embezzling the organization or trying to do something independently. That was worse. In a drug bust, you had rights, legal representation, a trial by jury. When Danny busted you, you went directly to sentencing, which was inevitably capital punishment, family or no family.

But it was true. Frankie wasn't greedy, at least when it came to Danny and the operation. Comfortable, even-tempered, optimistic—he enjoyed his life. He had been married and divorced twice, but he paid no alimony. With his second wife, Jackie, he had a son, Chipper, whom he was sending through law school, joking that he would have his personal mouthpiece soon. Recently, Frankie had met a new woman, Marilyn Chan, an ex–Las Vegas chorus girl. Her father was Chinese, but her mother was Italian. At forty-seven, she was still very attractive, with a drop-dead figure. He kept her on the payroll as a hostess. She had a great sense of humor, too.

"You know how an hour after you eat Chinese, you're hungry again?" he told his friends. "Well, an hour after Marilyn and me make love, we're at it again!"

"Don't believe him," she said. "He needs more than an hour."

Lots of laughter followed. There was always lots of laughter around Frankie Vico.

So life was good. He came to believe that he was really one of those chosen few born under a lucky star. Whatever difficulties and unpleasantness he had in his life, he had overcome with relatively minor damage. But then, suddenly, two days ago, while he was sitting in the restaurant enjoying some angel hair pasta, tomato, and basil, with a Diet Pepsi, his doctor called. Since Frankie had become health conscious, he had made it a point to have all the yearly exams. The last involved what he thought were routine chest X-rays. Dr. Reuben did not have good news.

"What does that mean, Doc?" Frankie said, wiping his lips clean.

"There might be something there, Mr. Vico," Dr. Reuben said. Frankie didn't want to comprehend.

"Something? Like what? Something I swallowed?"

"No, Mr. Vico. There's something of serious concern in your right lung."

"You're kidding."

"No, Mr. Vico. I'm sorry. We have to address this issue promptly."

"What? Lung cancer?"

He had been coughing on and off, but he ascribed that to an allergy.

"We need to do a lung biopsy in radiology. We'll use a CT scan," Dr. Reuben said. "I've arranged for you to have it this afternoon."

Frankie kept chewing. Across the room, Marilyn was laughing with a middle-aged tourist couple. She had no idea about the phone conversation he was having. She didn't even know he had gone for a checkup and blood tests.

Over by the entrance, sitting at his table, Frankie's right-hand man, Tony Marino, read the comics in the newspaper, chuckling gently, his jelly jowls trembling. He was six-foot-three, about forty pounds overweight, a heavy smoker and drinker, and, right now, as healthy as a horse. What about *his* lungs?

"You're kidding me. This afternoon?"

"The sooner the better for you, Mr. Vico," Dr. Reuben replied.

"Jesus. This is fucking unbelievable."

"I'm sorry," Dr. Reuben said, his voice growing thin and impatient. "But you want to get after these things as soon as possible. It could be nothing, some explainable shadows, perhaps."

"Maybe they read someone else's X-rays by mistake, huh?"

"The sooner we do the biopsy, the sooner we'll know if anything's cooking," Dr. Reuben said, without commenting on any such possibility. "All right?"

Frankie nodded.

"Mr. Vico?"

"Oh, yeah. Sure. Thanks," he replied. He heard the doctor hang up, but he held onto his receiver, driven by the urge to club someone to death with it just the way he had clubbed that creep Carlo Denardo to death with a tire iron in Los Angeles behind the Royal Flush club five years ago when he tried to stick him for three thousand after poker.

He cradled the phone slowly and walked over to Marilyn, who had just turned from the tourists.

"You ain't gonna believe this," he said. She smiled, waiting. Tony looked up from the comics. Frankie turned to him, too. "You ain't gonna fucking believe this."

"What's that, boss?"

"I might have lung cancer," he declared.

"What, Frankie?" Marilyn tossed her long black hair back over her shoulder. "You don't even smoke anymore," she said, "and I don't smoke, and there's no smoking in here."

He looked at her as if she were the queen of stupidity.

"Tony, get the fucking car. I gotta get over to the hospital right now," he ordered. Tony stared a moment too long. "NOW!" Frankie screamed.

Tony Marino wasn't normally a fast-moving man, but

anyone watching him get up and turn toward the door would think he was first cousin to Superman.

Joe Weber made the phone call right after speaking with Allan Parker. A man answered, and he assumed it was the donor's father.

"Mr. Petersen?"

"No," he said.

"Oh, I'm sorry. Is this 555-4434?"

"Yeah, but I ain't Mr. Petersen."

"Is there a Mr. Petersen or Mrs. Petersen at home? This is Doctor Weber," Joe said quickly.

"Mr. Petersen died. Heart attack years ago," Warren said dryly. "Mrs. Petersen's not home from work yet."

"Oh. Could you have her phone me when she gets in? If it's after five, my answering service will get a hold of me. The number's—"

"What's this about?" Warren demanded.

"Well, I have to speak with a member of the Petersen family. Are you—"

"I'm not related," Warren interrupted.

"I see. My number's 555-2322. I'm Jodi Walker's doctor," he added.

"Oh. How is she doing?"

"Tremendously," Joe said, not able to subdue his enthusiasm when it came to talking about Jodi Walker, even with someone he didn't know.

"Tremendously? What do you mean? Doesn't the kid have leukemia or something?"

"Not any longer," Joe said.

31

"She's better?"

"Completely. Please give Mrs. Petersen my message. Thank you," he added and hung up.

Warren shook his head, disdainfully thinking that doctors were so full of shit, and hung up the phone. Then he went to the refrigerator to get himself a beer. He had just sat down when Taylor entered, returning from school. The mother of his friend Jay Kasofsky drove him home. He and Jay were on the school's junior high debate team—something Warren ridiculed. When he gazed into the kitchen and saw Warren, he raised his head as a greeting but didn't say anything.

"Hey!" Warren called after Taylor had started away.

"What?"

"What's this about your cousin Jodi getting better?"

"Huh?"

"The doctor just called. Wants to talk to Demi. He said Jodi's all better."

Taylor stared at him with a smirk on his face. Surely Warren had gotten the message wrong.

"Didn't you go over to the hospital and donate blood?"

"Platelets and white cells," Taylor said.

"Ain't that blood?"

"It's in the blood." Since he was asked to donate them, and since Jodi needed them, he had looked up the pertinent information on his computer that night. "They're needed for blood clotting and to fight infections. If you don't have enough platelets, you could bleed to death."

"So if she's all better, why'd she need them?"

"Why don't you ask the doctor?" Taylor replied.

" 'Cause I'm asking you, Mr. Know-it-all. You're the debate team star, ain'tcha?"

"Well," Taylor said shrugging, not the least bit intimidated by Warren's gruff manner. "I guess I don't know it all." He remembered a Mark Twain joke the team used. "Actually, you and I know it all. I know everything there is to know, and you know the rest."

"What? That don't make any sense."

Taylor shrugged.

Even though he was dying to pour himself some cold milk and have an Oreo or two, he turned and walked away before Warren could figure out Twain's joke. He would wait until Warren left the kitchen. In the meantime, he retreated to his room and searched again on the computer to dig out more information on leukemia. He had just booted up when the phone rang. He and Warren picked it up at the same time.

"Oh, I'm so glad you're both there," Demi said.

"What's happening, Mom?" Taylor asked.

"Aunt Lois called. Jodi's made a miraculous recovery. The doctor said it was a miracle!"

"She's all better?"

"Yes, it looks that way."

"We heard. He called," Warren said.

"Who called, Warren?"

"The doctor. Left a number. He wants you to call him."

"Me? Why?"

"He wouldn't tell me because I'm not related."

"Smart doctor," Taylor said.

"Are you going to shut this kid up? Are you?"

"Taylor, please. What's his telephone number, Warren?"

Warren gave it to her.

"All right. I told Lois we would go out to celebrate with her and Ralph. Is that all right?"

"I hope this ain't no mistake," Warren said.

"You could always get a refund," Taylor quipped.

"I'll be home as soon as I can," Demi said quickly. "Be nice to each other. Please. Let's be happy. It's wonderful, just wonderful!"

Taylor returned to the computer and ran the search. He read about leukemia and sat back, wondering.

Maybe Warren was right. Maybe everyone misunderstood what the doctor was actually saying. He hoped and prayed not, mainly for Jodi's sake, of course, but also because it would be something else he could rub Warren's nose in, and that prospect was delightful.

Less than a half hour later, record time for Demi, she was at his door. From the look on her face, he assumed his suspicion was correct. It had been a mistake.

"She's not better?" he asked as soon as she had knocked and entered.

"No, she's better."

"So?"

"The doctor wants you come in to give him and the researchers a blood sample," she said.

"Researchers?"

"Yes, an important doctor is driving down from L.A."

"Really? Why?" His first thought was that they thought he had leukemia, too.

"They want to see if there was anything about your platelets and white blood cells that could have possibly . . ." The idea was so overwhelming she had trouble saying it.

"Possibly what?"

"Made her better."

Taylor sat back. Then he gazed at the computer screen where the words describing leukemia still lingered. Platelets corrected a symptom, not the disease, and white blood cells were needed when patients weren't responding to antibiotics. For attacking the cancer, there was only radiation, chemotherapy, bone marrow transplants . . . .

"That's dumb," he finally said.

"I know, but they really want to study your blood. Just to see, I suppose."

"Forget it," Taylor said. "I ain't getting stuck with needles again. I'm not a voodoo doll. Maybe the doctor's a vampire. Tell him to forget it, Mom."

She nodded.

"Okay, honey. Don't worry about it."

"I'm not worried. I just don't want to do it; that's all. They can't make me, right?"

"Right. Well," she said, smiling, "let's get ready to go to dinner with Aunt Lois and Uncle Ralph, okay?"

"Warren coming?"

"Sure," she said.

"He gonna pay for everyone?"

"I'll pay. It will be the happiest money I've spent in a long time," she said.

Taylor nodded. After she went downstairs to report

everything to Warren, Taylor sprawled on his bed and looked up at the ceiling. His father was unconscious in the ER the last time he had seen him. His eyes were closed, and already he looked like a corpse. Taylor recalled touching his father's arm just to see if he was still warm. Then he reached slowly for his father's long finger and held it for a moment.

That was his good-bye.

That was all the good-bye he had.

Why couldn't the doctors save him? Why couldn't the medicine work for him?

They don't know everything, he thought. They don't know anything.

But his mother said Jodi was better. It wasn't a mistake. How did they do it? Could it really have something to do with his blood?

He lifted his hand and followed the embossed vein along the inside of his wrist. The blood was flowing through him, doing its normal work. Nothing unusual was visible.

Why did they want to look at it under a microscope? It made him feel . . . freakish. Warren would just love that.

No, he wouldn't go back there. There was no point anyway. Jodi was better. Why wonder how come?

Let it be just a miracle, he thought. What's wrong with that?

"Naturally, we kept asking the doctor questions that amounted to the same one: Are you sure?" Lois said. She was crying with happiness, and Ralph was embarrassed but smiling. Warren ate as if it were going to be his last meal. Taylor envisioned a wild dog feasting on roadkill. It turned his stomach.

"Aren't you hungry, honey?" Demi asked him.

"Not as much as someone else here," he quipped, shifted his eyes to Warren, and then looked down at his food.

Warren stopped eating and looked at everyone. He took a deep breath, ashamed himself at how he was going at the food.

"This is damn good Risotto ai Funghi," he said in defense, and pumped his fork at his plate.

"Fungus? Doesn't that give you athlete's foot?" Taylor asked. He knew the answer but pretended he didn't.

Warren sat back and smirked.

"Fungi," Ralph said softly, "you know, are mushrooms, actually, Taylor. They're a delicacy, especially when they're made as well as this."

He had the same dish but was not anywhere as close to cleaning his plate as Warren was.

"Oh, yeah," Taylor said. "But I heard mushrooms could be poisonous."

"Not these," Ralph said, smiling. He knew what his nephew was doing.

Demi eyed Taylor angrily. She, too, knew he was quite aware of what fungi were. He was just teasing Warren. She poked him gently with her knee, and he started to eat.

"Look," Warren said, returning to his food, "I don't want to throw cold water on anything, but how could your daughter be so sick and cured practically in hours? Did you ask the doctor that?"

"Of course we did, Warren," Lois said. "He showed us the lab results, and he showed us how he had reconfirmed everything. He wasn't the only one looking at the results."

"That's why I'd rather not go to a hospital. Billy Morris's father nearly had his gall bladder removed before someone noticed the doctor was given the wrong test results. And Gerry Marcus's uncle Pete is still fighting the damn staph infection he got in the hospital. Nearly killed him. Your daughter probably had the flu or something," Warren added.

No one spoke for a moment. Then Demi smiled.

"Whatever the reason, we're all grateful Jodi's well and coming home."

"When is she coming home?" Warren asked.

"The doctor wanted to keep her for observation another forty-eight hours."

"Maybe we're celebrating too soon," Warren muttered.

"Warren!" Demi cried and then softened her lips to a smile.

"I just hate doctors," he said. "And disappointments."

"Your poor mother," Taylor countered.

Warren's mouth dropped. But Lois and Ralph couldn't hold back laughter.

"This kid's going to either write comedy or perform it," Ralph added to soften their amusement at Warren's expense.

Warren's red face darkened, and he threw down his fork.

"I need a cigarette," he said, rising. He would have to go outside to light up.

No one, not even Demi, tried to talk him out of it. As everyone continued to eat, he strolled out.

"I don't think Warren appreciates your sense of humor, Taylor," his uncle Ralph said.

"He hasn't quite learned how to think before he speaks yet," Demi said, giving Taylor her big-eyed look of reprimand.

"Sorry," Taylor told her. She was very upset now and he didn't want to be the cause of unhappiness at this celebration.

"Don't tell me. Tell Warren," she ordered. "Do it," she ordered firmly.

"Now?"

"It's always better to apologize as soon as possible when you do something unpleasant, Taylor," she advised.

He nodded and stood up. Then he smiled.

"That explains it," he said.

"Explains what?" his aunt Lois asked.

"Why the doctor told his mother he was sorry seconds after he delivered Warren," he replied.

There was a moment of hesitation, but as he started away from the table, the three adults burst into laughter behind him. He smiled to himself and walked out of the restaurant to find Warren.

He was standing off to the right, smoking and looking out at the Palm Springs Tram light clearly visible at the top of the mountains. The tram carried tourists to nearly 11,000 feet where which they could see incredible views or take hikes.

"Sorry if I insulted you," Taylor said.

Warren turned and looked at him.

"Your mother send you out here?"

"It wasn't Federal Express," Taylor replied.

"You got a big trap on you, kid. I'm not sure how much longer I'm going to put up with it."

"When you find out, let me know," Taylor told him.

"Oh, don't worry about that, Taylor. You'll be the first," Warren said, stepping toward him. He glared down at him. "You're a spoiled little bastard, and sooner or later, you're going to get your head handed to you. Maybe it won't be me and maybe it will. We'll see how smart you are then."

A number of smart replies streamed through Taylor's mind, but he checked each one at the tip of his tongue and turned away instead. He sensed the danger. Warren was capable of great violence.

As he approached the table, his mother, aunt, and uncle looked up with expectation.

"So?" Demi asked when he sat.

"It went over real well. We're going to be pals. He promised to share his monthly allotment of arsenic with me," Taylor quipped and began to eat again as if his appetite had returned in spades.

Demi and Lois looked at each other. Lois smiled, and Demi shook her head. They all looked up when Warren returned. He was quiet but ordered another drink. Ralph tried to start a conversation about the new shopping center being proposed in Palm Springs. As the accountant involved with the developer, he thought he might get

Warren work. Warren was skeptical about its being approved.

"Everything's going down valley," he said. "Forget Palm Springs."

Taylor smiled to himself. He had just thought, Why don't you? He clamped down on it quickly but couldn't wipe off his smile fast enough. Warren glared at him, and Ralph tried getting him back to the discussion by giving him some inside information.

"It's going to happen," he concluded. "Good things," he added, nodding at everyone. "Good things coming all around."

That was enough to bring back the good mood. Warren relaxed with his drink and even began looking at Demi with some sexual promises in his eyes. She blushed but felt better and even hopeful.

We'll be a family yet, she thought. We've got to be.

CHAPTER TWO

"I'm sorry. What did you say?" Allan asked. He pulled on his earlobe like Humphrey Bogart and spoke through his bluetooth phone in the car as he sped along the 10 Freeway east to Palm Springs. "You said the boy's mother said he doesn't want to come in and therefore she won't come in?"

"That's what I said, Allan. It's not like we can issue a summons," Joe replied.

Allan was quiet for a moment.

"You're sure about all your facts? The timetable here, all of it?"

"C'mon, Allan. I wouldn't have taken the time to call you. I know how busy you are, too."

"I'm just asking. It's normal to ask these questions under the circumstances you're describing."

"Yes, it's normal once, twice, but not eight times. I'm sure."

"Then we've got to get him to come in, Joe. I need that sample."

"*We* need the sample," Joe corrected.

"That's what I mean. We need the sample."

42

"I still don't understand what you're expecting to find here, Allan."

"I'll go into detail when I see you. You have their address?"

"What are you going to do, make him an offer he can't refuse? He's a fifteen-year-old kid."

"Tell me more about him, his family," Allan said.

"I just found out about them myself, only because I have the village gossip as a receptionist in my office," Joe said. "The boy's mother works in a beauty salon. His father died of a heart attack a little over two years ago. She's now living with a man who works construction."

"Heart attack, huh?"

"On the job."

"What did he do?"

"He was a computer programmer but worked at Palo Alto for a considerable time before they moved here."

"Palo Alto? You don't mean he had anything to do with the nuclear energy facility there, do you?"

"I think so. I think that's what she said."

"You know they had an incident there nearly sixteen, seventeen years ago?"

"No, I didn't know. Maybe I did but forgot," Joe quickly corrected. He didn't want to appear to be totally oblivious to news events, even though he was.

"We've had more than a half dozen cases of a variety of cancer illnesses involving employees who worked there and were exposed to radiation at the time. This is even more interesting now."

"What are you reaching for here, Allan?" Joe asked.

He could almost hear his friend's thoughts. He did hear some new excitement in his voice.

"I'm about an hour away, Joe. See what details about him your receptionist can get for us."

"Allan, look, the mother was pretty clear about the boy's refusal and . . ."

"I'll be there in an hour. Try to get the details. It's important, Joe. I'll explain more when I get there. There is something going on at a research center in North Carolina involving mice. I'll get into it when we get together. It has a lot of people excited," he said and shut off his phone.

Could this be? He felt like a young boy about to go to his first party. He couldn't contain the excitement raging in his body and didn't realize until it was too late that he had accelerated to 110 miles an hour.

The highway patrolman hitting traffic on the 10 Freeway with his radar gun was actually so enraged that he stalled his motorcycle in his rush to go after him. He cursed and got started. First, the patrolman hated having to go this speed himself. He wasn't comfortable about it even though he had been a motorcycle patrolman for nearly ten years. Second, usually when a driver saw him coming with his flashing lights, he slowed his vehicle and began to pull to the side, but this driver was either a criminal or simply oblivious. Whatever the case, this was damn serious. He got on his radio and called for backup. He was closing on 100 miles an hour, and the driver still hadn't indicated he was going to slow down.

"This guy's going to jail," he swore and accelerated.

It wasn't until the motorcycle patrolman pulled alongside his vehicle that Allan realized he was being pursued. The policeman was gesturing emphatically for him to pull over, so he raised his hand to indicate he understood and slowed down.

It never occurred to him during the last five minutes that there was anyone else in the world.

Almost as soon as he pulled over to a stop, he saw a highway patrol car in his rearview mirror, speeding in his direction. The motorcycle cop appeared to be waiting as well. The cop dismounted and unbuckled his pistol.

"What the hell's going on?" Allan asked, peering.

The patrol car pulled up in front, and two officers got out quickly, their guns drawn, their doors open to shield them.

"Step out of your vehicle," he heard, "and put your hands on your head."

"Holy Christmas," Allan muttered and did as he was told. Then he was told to face the car.

The motorcycle cop reached him first and pulled his hands down to cuff him.

"What's going on?"

"You're going on—to jail," the cop replied. "That's what's going on."

"For speeding?"

"You were going 110 miles an hour and did not respond to my pursuit."

The other two officers holstered their weapons and walked slowly to him.

"I'm sorry," Allan said. "I was in very deep thought."

"Deep enough to bury yourself," the unsympathetic motorcycle cop said. "Your registration in your car?"

"Yes, sir. Glove compartment."

"License in your wallet?"

"Inside jacket pocket," Allan said. He started to turn, and the motorcycle cop stopped him roughly. One of the patrolmen from the police car reached into his pocket and produced his wallet. He opened it to look at his identification.

"You have a doctor here, Gerry," he said. He continued to explore the cards. "Out of U.S.C. Oncology."

The news seemed to calm the motorcycle cop somewhat.

"Why were you going so fast?" he demanded.

"Can I turn?"

"Turn around."

Allan faced the nearly square-jawed policeman. He wore very dark sunglasses and had a solid-looking body, too. Allan could see himself in the sunglass lenses. For a flashing moment, Allan thought of a comic book character and nearly smiled. At this moment he realized that would be disastrous.

"I'm on my way to the hospital in Palm Springs. I am in cancer research, and there's an extraordinary case there that could have something to do with my work."

How do I go much further, he thought, without getting far too technical and sounding condescending?

"It's gotten me excited," he added.

The three policemen looked at each other.

46

"I was in deep thought about that and frankly didn't even realize how fast I was traveling."

"Yeah, well, I'm not as smart as an oncologist, but I *can* figure out what might happen if I blew a tire at that speed."

"Absolutely. I've been accused of being an absent-minded professor. I stand guilty to the charge."

The motorcycle cop smirked.

"Turn around," he said, and Allan did so quickly. He heard and felt him unlocking the handcuffs.

"That's a first for me," Allan told him as he rubbed his reddened wrists.

"Yeah, well, we're not taking you to jail, Doc, but I'm going to give you a pretty serious speeding ticket, so I hope you have a good lawyer."

Allan didn't respond.

"Hey, Gerry," the patrolman who had his wallet said. "Can I speak to you a minute?"

The motorcycle cop didn't reply. He just walked a few feet away with the other patrolman, and they conferred. Allan took a deep breath and now risked smiling at the third patrolman, who just stared at him.

The two returned, the one patrolman handing him back his wallet and then his registration.

"You're about twenty minutes out if you go the speed limit, Doc," the patrolman who had taken his wallet said.

He looked at the motorcycle cop, who said nothing. Allan nodded and got into his car. The patrolmen from the highway patrol car began walking back to theirs. Allan started his engine, and the motorcycle cop knocked on his window. He lowered it quickly.

"Cory's mother is in chemotherapy. Breast cancer. I'm doing this for her," he said. "Watch yourself," he warned and headed for his motorcycle.

Allan let out a deep, hot breath, put his car into drive, and pulled away slowly. He glanced at the patrolman at the wheel of the patrol car and then looked forward.

Everyone is praying for the same magic bullet, he thought. He had contradictory feelings. He was proud of what he was doing and how much respect it garnered, but he was also ashamed that he had escaped a speeding ticket only because a man's mother was dying from cancer.

"I hate it!" he screamed. "I hate it!"

He pounded the wheel. Anyone driving by would think he was clearly losing his mind.

He stopped himself, took a deep breath and drove on.

Two bowlers throwing perfect strikes simultaneously on side-by-side alleyways created an explosion of sound that echoed through the building and interrupted Frankie Vico's conversation at his bar. He was leaning over and lecturing his new bartender about moving quicker to get more booze in the glasses and more dollars in the register.

"Your eyes got to be on the glasses, not the drinkers," he emphasized. He tapped the bar with his cigarette lighter in the shape of a pen. Although he had stopped smoking, he liked carrying it. "Maybe nowhere else in any business is time as much money as it is in a bar, Stuart.

Every glass on the bar is like a parking meter. The moment it looks empty, boom!" he cried. "You put in more. If they stop you, they stop you. Most will appreciate it and so will my cash register. Capiche?"

"Got it," Stuart Blockman said. He just wanted this to end, and it seemed like it wouldn't in his lifetime. Frankie had such hot, bad breath that when he spoke, it was like a blowtorch coming over the bar at him. Plus, the only reason he liked bartending was the contact he had with people, not glasses. Sure, time was money here, but it was the connection the bartender made with his customers that kept the customers coming and spending money. How come Frankie didn't see that?

"There's big overhead here, Stuart. I got this bowling alley and the restaurant under one roof, yes, but the taxes, the employees, the utilities . . . they're killers if we don't fill the glasses constantly. I make more here at this bar in an hour than I do on those alleyways in a day."

"But the bowling brings them here," Stuart made the mistake of saying. That only got Frankie off on another tangent: the inflationary costs associated with a bowling alley in today's economy, which then took him onto politics.

Stuart looked toward Frankie's new girlfriend, Marilyn Chan, hoping she would soon call him back to the table where Frankie's goon, Tony Marino, sat reading a comic book. She saw his look of desperation, shrugged her shoulders and smiled. She's torturing me, Stuart thought. But he dared not utter a syllable of complaint. He knew this whole enterprise was basically a laundering operation for Frankie's cocaine business. Who didn't know it, except apparently the law enforcement agencies? Maybe they did but were paid off. Who was he to say? Hear no evil. Speak no evil. And live.

The ringing of the telephone was like a lifeline thrown his way by Verizon. He nodded his head in its direction, and Frankie stopped talking.

"Get the fucking phone," he ordered, acting like Stuart should have just walked away when it rang, when Stuart knew in his heart that if he had done that, Frankie would have been pissed and you don't piss off Frankie Vico.

"Strike Zone, Stuart speaking," Stuart said into the phone. He looked at Frankie to see if that greeting was all right and listened. "Yes, he's right here. It's for you, Frankie," he said. "Doctor Reuben's office."

"Give me the damn phone," Frankie said. He looked back at the table and saw Marilyn was doing her fingernails at the table. He hated that and had told her again just that morning, too.

Stuart brought the phone to the bar and stepped back as if he were afraid it might explode in his face.

"Vico," Frankie said. He listened. "Oh, yeah, I'll hold."

He put his hand over the receiver.

"Don't stand there looking at me. Get those glasses clean, Stuart."

"Right."

Frankie returned to the receiver.

"Hey, Doc. What?"

As he listened, he felt the blood draining from his face.

"You sure?" Even his neck grew white now. "Yeah, sure. I'll go right over to see him. You're absolutely sure? I mean, everything was checked and double-checked, right? Yeah. Okay. Thanks," he said and slammed the receiver down so hard on the cradle it nearly cracked. "I gotta take a ride," he shouted at Tony. The goon folded the comic book quickly and stood up.

"Where are you going now, Frankie?" Marilyn asked, annoyed.

"Another doctor's office. My bopsy wasn't good."

She stopped filing her nails for a moment. "What's a bopsy?" she asked.

Frankie started out.

"Jesus, Marilyn, I've told you a hundred times. Don't do your nails in the restaurant. Shit," he said. He continued cursing anything and everything as he followed Tony out to the car.

When he got in, Tony just sat there waiting. Frankie looked at him.

"Where we going, boss?"

"Where we going? Maybe hell," Frankie said.

Anyone else but me might feel damn foolish doing this, Allan thought, as he drove up to Demi Petersen's house. He had just spent more than two hours reviewing Joe's patient's miraculous recovery, and he could come up with no logical medical explanation except the one he had tracked recently to research with mice. A strain of cancer-resistant mice had been discovered, and when their white blood cells had been transfused to mice with tumors, the tumors immediately were gone. To date, as far as he knew, there was no human experiment with similar results.

When he'd called the Petersens, he got the answering machine. He left his cell phone number and then went to dinner with Joe and his wife Toby. He tried to be good company, but had difficulty treating any topic of conversation as interesting or important and was especially bored with domestic topics. Toby clearly was growing more and more annoyed and flashed her irritation at Joe periodically. Allan continually checked his cell phone, worried that the volume wasn't high enough to hear a call or that the signal was too weak inside the restaurant.

"Maybe they don't want to call you back, Allan," Toby suggested. "They already gave Joe an answer, and now you're calling for the same reason. You can't stalk them. How do you intend to get them to agree?"

"I'll make them an offer they can't refuse," he said. "Like a medical godfather."

Toby laughed. But Allan didn't laugh. He didn't smile.

"Are you serious?" she asked. Joe froze his smile. "What, money?"

"From what Joe's told me about them, they're not exactly rolling around in money."

"Is that ethical?"

"Sure. We pay people to donate their blood, don't we?" Allan replied before Joe could respond.

"He's right. This isn't exactly the same thing, but . . ."

"It's not. It's far more important," Allan insisted.

Toby had made the mistake of giving him the lead-in.

He went on and on, practically repeating a paper he had recently done for a convention of oncologists, spewing off statistics. She began to sink in a pool of regret and boredom and was actually grateful when Allan's phone sounded. He nearly leaped out of his seat, nodded at them to indicate it was Demi Petersen, and walked away to talk.

A little more than a minute later, he returned, his face full of excitement.

"The mother will see me right now," he said. "They were out to dinner."

He peeled off some money, but Joe wouldn't let him pay anything.

"Just go," he said. "I'll wait up for you."

"Right. Right," he babbled and went off.

"Finally," Toby said, watching Allan leave the restaurant, "we can relax."

Allan was impatient with his GPS until it outlined the route to the Petersens' home. A lot more conscious about his driving since he was pulled over on the freeway, he drove slower than he would have liked. He was encouraged by the modest two-story home with only a suggestion of a front lawn and faded wood panels fencing it off from the neighboring houses and properties. Money should be important to them, he thought as he got out of his vehicle and walked toward the front door. Before he reached it, Demi opened it to greet him. She had put on a tight-knit light-green dress for the dinner celebration and looked quite attractive.

For some reason Allan had envisioned an older, harder-looking woman. He was actually hoping she'd be that way. Attractive women took him off his game.

"Doctor Parker?"

She had a very soft, comforting smile. It actually worked well for him, calming him down.

"Yes. Thanks for agreeing to see me on such short notice," he said. "But I just drove in today and—"

"Please, come in."

Demi led him into the living room. It was a very modest home inside as well, but decorated with some good taste. His eyes caught the cigarette butts pressed into a piece of cardboard on a table beside the sofa, however. There was other evidence of someone's sloppiness: a pair of men's slippers under the coffee table, a flannel shirt tossed over the back of the sofa, and a nearly empty beer bottle on a side table.

"Would you like something to drink? Alcoholic or not?"

"No, thank you."

"Hey, are you the hotshot from L.A.?" Allan heard and turned.

"This is Warren Moore," Demi said when Warren came in from the kitchen. She didn't explain anymore about him, but Allan assumed he was her significant other and shook hands quickly. His father had taught him not to have a limp grip when shaking another man's hand and it stood in his mind. Warren was obviously surprised.

"Hardly a hotshot." Allen turned back to Demi. "I'm

really sorry about coming over this late, but I felt it was really important, and I hope before I'm finished explaining, you will see it that way, too."

"Please, have a seat," Demi said. She looked at Warren, who already appeared bored and disinterested. When he lit a cigarette, Allan glared.

"Warren, maybe Doctor Parker would rather not sit with someone smoking."

"Oh, no . . . it's . . ."

"Fine. I'll be outside," Warren said sullenly and left.

She looked after him sadly but then smiled at Allan.

"I don't mean to intrude," he said.

"Go on, Doctor Parker. I'm sorry. Warren's one of those men who doesn't like to be told to do anything, and I'm a Sagittarius. We don't hide our thoughts. Don't ask me how we manage to get along. It's a mystery."

Allan laughed, admiring her for being able to be humorous and laid back about her relationship.

He gave her his resume as quickly and as simply as he could. He had already decided that the best way to peel this onion was to get her to think of her niece and relate that to other children who were in similar states. She looked moved, especially when he described the twelve-year-old he was about to lose.

"I admire you for all that wonderful work you do, but I don't know how you can stand the tragedies."

"It's like that famous saying, 'What doesn't destroy you makes you stronger.'"

"Nietzsche."

"Yes," Allan said, impressed.

Demi laughed.

"I don't know anything more than that. My son mumbles that expression all the time and told me it comes from Nietzsche."

"Your son?"

She nodded, proudly, and then grew serious. "Despite all you've explained, I'm still not sure I understand why you want my son to give more of his blood, Doctor Parker."

"Well, I reviewed your niece's case, and to be absolutely frank, Mrs. Petersen . . ."

"Demi, please."

"Demi. There is no medical explanation we know at the moment that would explain why your niece is still alive tonight. More importantly, why she is in this complete remission so quickly. There has been, however, a fascinating experiment involving mice."

Warren returned just as Allan finished his last remark.

"Mice, huh? Taylor reminds me of a little mouse sometimes," he offered and laughed. Demi didn't even smile.

"Doctor Parker is just finishing his explanation, Warren," she said, eyeing the sofa and clearly telling him to shut up.

Warren nodded, still not looking interested, but slipped onto the sofa to sit beside her.

"As I was saying, this experiment was with mice, only not usual mice. These mice appear to be cancer resistant. Their white blood cells, when transplanted into mice that were given what should have been lethal doses of highly aggressive new cancers, not only killed the existing cancer but protected the mice against the new, more lethal doses, and it all happened relatively rapidly.

"I don't want to get too technical, but it has to do with white blood cells that attack the cancer cells—all sorts of cancer, by the way."

Demi just stared.

Warren smiled and sat up.

"So I was right. The kid's got mouse blood or something, huh?"

"No," Allan said, seeing the man was actually trying to be serious. "He can't have the same blood, but the interaction suggests that what provided the cancer resistance in the mice might occur in human beings, if there were such a donor. This is the first case that suggests it, to my knowledge, that is."

"So you think there's something about Taylor's blood that's cancer resistant?" Demi asked.

"Exactly," Allan said.

"Why his blood?" Warren asked, looking more angry than interested.

"I can only theorize at this stage, but it might have something to do with the dosage of radiation Mr. Petersen experienced. This occurred before your son was conceived, correct, Mrs. Petersen?" For some reason, he found it difficult calling her Demi with Warren present.

"Yes. And Buddy never came down with any form of

cancer, although he heard that some of his coworkers had. We were always expecting it. Concerned about every ache or pain. It was truly like living with a . . ."

"Sword over your head?"

"Exactly."

Allan nodded, smiling, trying to contain his excitement. She was far from an ignorant woman. He grew more confident. He could get through to someone like her.

"I don't get it. What sword?" Warren asked.

"It's just an expression. It means living with something threatening," she said.

The way she looked at him made his face turn a shade of crimson. Allan couldn't help but pick up a negative vibration. He couldn't help wondering what she was doing with this man. He chalked it up to the female temperament. That was an even bigger mystery to him than cancer, and always had been.

"Actually, this is why I'm even more interested in what's occurred vis-à-vis Taylor's blood donation. We had some of those cases of cancer you're referring to that initiated out of Palo Alto, so I know about the dosage they experienced. It was very significant."

"And the kid might have something special about his blood because of that?" Warren asked quickly.

Allan nodded. He preferred to direct himself to Demi.

"If that's all true, this kid is a walking gold mine," Warren added.

"I can't be so quick to say something like that," Allan told him in a far more formal tone. "There's a lot to be done before anything could be confirmed, but step one is to get another sample of his blood—those white cells to be precise and—"

"What's it worth?" Warren pursued.

Allan looked at him. "You can't possibly put a price on something like this, Mr . . ."

"Moore. Priceless. I love it," Warren said smiling.

Demi suddenly looked upset, however. Allan realized he might be overwhelming and frightening her with his rabid enthusiasm. He tried to calm down and speak more nonchalantly.

"To pursue these possibilities, I just need a small sample. It won't take long. But," he added quickly, "I can understand the child's reluctance. Who likes to give blood?"

"Women, once a month," Warren joked.

"Jesus, Warren," Demi said.

"I'm just trying to lighten things up," he said. "I don't see why it ain't worth something if it's so damn important."

"Maybe, if you agree, of course, we could . . . I mean I could give your son a thousand dollars towards his college education," Allan offered.

"A thousand dollars!" Warren leaned forward. "For what? How much blood?"

"Not any more than you would give for routine blood tests," Allan said.

Clearly attracted to the proposal, Warren looked at Demi.

"I'll talk to Taylor about all this in the morning," she said. "He's gone to sleep."

"For a thousand bucks, you can wake him up."

"I'd rather sleep on it myself and talk to him in the morning, if that's all right with you, Doctor Parker," she said, firmly enough for Allan to realize he had gone as far as he could.

"Jesus," Warren said shaking his head. "She works two weeks for a thousand dollars and she's getting that carpet tunnel syndrome."

"Carpal tunnel, Warren."

"Whatever. She breathes in all those damn chemicals they put on hair these days, too, not to mention the garbage she has to take from some of those women who would look better if someone took a blowtorch to them."

"Warren, please. Dr. Parker doesn't have to hear all that."

"I'm okay with you sleeping on it, Mrs. Petersen," Allan said, standing. "You have my number. I'll be at Doctor Weber's office in the morning, and then I'll be at the hospital to participate in your niece's final run-through," he said.

"Is she still okay?" Warren asked.

"She's fine. That's why I've come from Los Angeles. We have something going on here that's quite unusual but might be quite promising for lots of children like Jodi."

Warren slapped his hands together and stood.

"Thanks for stopping by, Doc," he said, extending his hand.

Allan shook it, forced a smile, and started for the front

entrance. Demi followed him out the door and closed it softly behind her.

"I'm not the smartest woman you're going to meet, Doctor Parker. I'm not the best mother a child's ever had either, but I have some pretty good motherly, female instincts."

"Sure," Allan said. "I . . ."

"If what you're thinking, hoping, is even possible and my son is this amazing . . . I don't know . . . good freak or something, this could have some very serious consequences for him. I mean, ironically, I'd be afraid for him."

"I understand," Allan said and reached down inside himself for his best bedside manner. "Listen, Demi, I lost my mother to breast cancer. I've devoted my life to the pursuit of cancer cures. My associates call me Doctor Sisyphus behind my back. I know they do. He was a character in Greek mythology who was forced to do just one thing over and over. I admit I'm obsessed, but it's a good obsession. I'm sort of a monk, only I'm dedicated to the worship of science—science that can do something miraculous. I'm not religious in any sense, but I accept the possibility that God works his miracles through us, through science, in fact.

"That's about as corny as I can get," he added, smiling, and then grew deadly serious, "but I can tell you this, no one would be more protective of your son than I would be. I'd make sure of that. Damn sure.

"One last thing," he said as he stepped away and turned. "I meant what I said in there. There are thousands of children whose parents will not have the morning after that your sister and her husband are having."

She watched him get into his car. He looked back at her and smiled to himself. She hadn't just turned away and gone back inside. His words nailed her.

I did it, he thought with a twinge of guilt. He would have liked to have taken more time with her. She was a pretty nice woman, but that Neanderthal made him rush his approach.

Confident, he drove quietly back to the Webers' house, continuing to think about Demi Petersen more than he had expected he would.

This isn't the time to contemplate romantic thoughts, Allan Parker, he told himself.

"He's in the living room," Toby Weber said as soon as Allan entered. "I was just going to bed. See you in the morning," she added, turned quickly, and walked off. He was surprised at her apparent indifference, but Joe was obviously just waiting for Allan's return. He could see the interest in his eyes.

He's as eager for this as I am, Allan thought happily when he saw him.

"What was it like?" he asked quickly.

"She's very nice, but she's living with this kindergarten dropout who bulldozed his way into the conversation. He didn't hesitate to demand money."

"Really?"

"I offered her a thousand dollars to put toward her son's education."

"And?"

"I think I did a pretty good presentation, considering. She's bright. She understood what I was saying."

"Okay. She's nice and she's bright, and you offered her a thousand dollars. So, did she agree?"

"Not yet," he replied. "But she will."

CHAPTER THREE

Allan had trouble sleeping. It bothered him that he kept remembering little things about Demi Petersen's face, like the way she lifted her upper lip just slightly when she went into a deeper thought or raised her right eyebrow when he became just a little too animated. It helped him put the brakes on a bit, but none of this should be on his mind now, he kept telling himself.

He had sat up with Joe talking about some of their previous cases and the research with which they were both familiar. He drank a little more than he had intended and did finally fall asleep, but he woke a little more than an hour later and tossed and turned the rest of the night, sometimes thinking about Demi Petersen and then reviewing data and dreaming of how he would go forward if this proved to be what it appeared to be. He was never one to sleep too many hours anyway. Ever since his intern days, he did well with four, maybe five hours. He knew the importance of sleep, but he was intolerant of it. Cancer didn't sleep, did it?

"How's your young patient?" he asked immediately upon entering the kitchen. He had had the terrible thought that the miraculous remission would be gone after another night had passed.

Joe was at the table sipping some coffee and glancing at the newspaper. Allan knew he had checked in with the hospital the moment he rose.

"Terrific. I've decided to release her today. There's nothing more we can do for her or need to do. What would you like for breakfast? Toby's taken the kids to school."

"Great. I'll have some of that cold cereal and fruit you have out, thanks," he said and poured the cereal into a bowl. After he sat, he put his phone on the table. Joe looked at it.

"I know how confident you were last night, Allan, but what if she doesn't call?"

"I'll raise the offer until she does. What else am I going to do with my money?" he replied, smiling, and ate.

"I have to tell you, Allan, I'm not sure what I would do in her shoes. I understand her concerns."

"Hey, so do I, and I meant what I said. I'll make sure that kid is protected. Who else even knows we're thinking about all this?"

"You know that saying about a secret. Two can keep it if one is dead. It's a bit late to contain it. From the way you described her boyfriend, I wouldn't count on discretion."

"One step at a time, Joe. Something's here. I feel it, and so do you."

Joe nodded. "I can't explain it any other way," he admitted.

It was enough for Allan. His eyes lit up with anticipation. Anyone not knowing his monomania would think he was high on some hallucinogenic. Sometimes, Joe thought Allan might be better off if he were. At least then there was the possibility of rehabilitation.

By the time they reached the hospital, Demi had still not called, and Allan was getting nervous. What if he hadn't been as persuasive as he thought and money couldn't buy them? He went with Joe on his rounds, but he wasn't as much help as he could have been. His mind was elsewhere. He did go with him to sign out Jodi Walker and meet her parents. After Joe introduced them, Allan mentioned he had visited Demi, and Lois confessed that her sister had called her in the morning.

"Oh?"

"She's conflicted about it. Give her a little more time," Lois said.

Allan nodded and wished them all luck when they headed out with Jodi. He saw the glow in Joe's face, too.

What would it be like if I could release my patients like this? he thought. His anxiety was quickly turning into subdued rage. Why wasn't the money enough? He was asking for so little. He was nearly beside himself and even contemplated returning to Los Angeles when his phone finally rang.

"I'll bring him around after school," Demi Petersen said. "To Doctor Weber's office. I'd rather we did it there than at the hospital."

"Oh, absolutely," Allan said. "No problem. What time is after school?"

"I should be there with Taylor about three thirty, if that's all right."

"Perfect," Allan said. She could have said any time she wanted, and he would have said, "perfect."

"I'd like you to explain it better to my son. He's very bright. I don't want him to feel freakish or anything."

"Oh, I will. He can even be there in the lab, if he wants, when I run some initial tests."

"I don't think that'll be necessary, but thank you."

"And I'll have the money for him."

She didn't respond. He sensed she wanted to say it wasn't necessary, but he imagined her boyfriend harping on it so much that she had no choice. He started to feel sorry for her and then stopped himself. This isn't the time to get into the middle of someone's soap opera, he told himself. His goal was to save lives. How people wasted or improved those lives afterward was not his business. After all, he was a scientist, not a therapist.

He hurried to tell Joe, who became amused with Allan's anticipation. He was like an expectant father until three thirty, pacing, looking dumbly at television, making some routine phone calls, and hating the minute hand on the clock for taking so long to move.

He worked on keeping himself calm and casual. He didn't want to spook the kid or his mother any more than they were, especially after Demi Petersen had implied that the kid was feeling freakish. Finally, they arrived. He could see the deep worry in Demi Petersen's face, but he was surprised and grateful for the coolness in the boy and the insight inherent in Taylor's first question.

"How do you know it was my blood cells that did anything? She had transplants from other donors, right? Maybe whatever happened took longer than you think," Taylor said.

Allan smiled at him. In his own mind, Taylor Petersen had already achieved superhuman status, so it was easy to see in him a superior intelligence and a wisdom in his eyes that went far beyond his chronological age. In many ways, in fact, Taylor reminded Allan of himself. He seemed to have the same alertness, awareness, and depth of perception that fed on distrust. Skepticism and doubt led to more intense evaluation and brought up questions the trusting mind never imagines.

"Nothing is for certain yet, Taylor, but there is a cause and effect relationship to evaluate," he replied. "Some mechanism triggered all this pretty quickly."

Allan winked at Demi, who started to relax. He was determined to make a hit with the kid and win over his confidence, but he couldn't help enjoying the effect his treating Taylor like an adult had on Demi as well. She gave him a nice smile, maybe initiated by more than simple appreciation. He was surprised at how much he wanted that to be true.

"The time period between the other transfusions and yours is significant enough for us to focus on you," he added. "Understand, buddy?"

Taylor shrugged. "You're the doctor."

Allan laughed and again looked at Demi, who was holding those beautiful lips of hers just a shade or two away from a brighter smile. It was clear how much she enjoyed and loved her son.

"Sometimes, I have to keep telling myself that, Taylor." He turned back to Demi. "I saw from Taylor's medical history that he has been pretty healthy. He didn't miss a day of school last year?"

"You got his medical history?"

"Oh, yes," Allan said, fumbling for the right words. "We have to consider everything. I mean . . ."

She nodded.

"He likes going to school," Demi said. "He'd go even if he didn't feel well."

Allan nodded and smiled.

"I went a year without missing a day, too. Cut a few when I started college," he said, winking at Taylor.

"Some of my teachers wouldn't know if I was there or not," Taylor said, and Allan laughed.

"I had a few of those, too."

"How'd you stay awake?"

"I'm not sure I did." Allan hurriedly prepared the needle but tried not to look too determined.

"I count 'er's," Taylor told him.

" 'Er's?"

"You know, when they go 'er' before they say something, or in the middle of a sentence. Mr. Hunter broke the record recently. Two hundred and two 'er's in one day."

Joe Weber roared with laughter. Allan smiled and shook his head.

"You have quite a kid here," he told Demi.

"I know," she said. "Sometimes, too quite."

Allan drew the first tube, practically salivating as the blood poured in.

"You gonna check my neutrophils and macrophages?" Taylor asked as Allan hurriedly attached the second tube to the needle.

Allan's eyebrows nearly flew off his head.

"He's always on the computer," Demi said. "When he gets onto a subject, he won't let go until he learns everything he can about it. He's always been that way. Full of questions."

"Why do you say that, Mom?" Taylor asked, and she, Allan, and Joe laughed.

"Getting back to your question, Taylor, we are going to check your neutrophils and macrophages," Allan said. "The research done emphasizes those cells."

He turned to Demi.

"The combine system of white blood cells forms a first line of host defense against pathogens, such as bacteria," he told her. "Preliminary studies show that the white blood cells under examination can also kill endogenous cancers, cancers that spring up naturally from the body's own cells. There are those who believe we're all living with cancer cells, and when the immune system falters, those cells dominate."

"Like a weakness in a fortress?" Taylor added.

"Exactly," Allan said. "We might have a future doctor here," he added, slipping on the third tube.

Allan saw that Demi look impressed with him.

"Doctor Parker has become something of a superstar

in the battle against cancer," Joe said with pride. "If he thinks that about Taylor, it means something."

"I think I want to be an astronaut," Taylor said. "There are too many people I'd rather look down on than up to."

Both he and Joe roared again.

"My money's on him no matter what he wants to do," Allan said. He watched the tube fill and then added the fourth.

"How many of those are you doing?" Demi asked.

"They need four," Taylor replied before Allan could.

"He's right. Almost done."

Demi's smile was softer, warmer, but he saw there was still great anxiety in that pretty face. He concentrated on finishing the job and then had Joe's nurse quickly bandage Taylor. He put the tubes safely in a packet. Afterward, as surreptitiously as he could manage, he handed Demi an envelope with the check for $1000, but he sensed Taylor had caught sight of it.

"This wasn't my idea," Demi said, not hiding her embarrassment.

Allan smiled. "I know," he said. "But that's fine. It's worth it to me. We're going to get right on this," he told her. "As soon as we have some definitive result, I'll call you, but it could be quite a long time."

She nodded. Taylor had his hands in his pockets and was standing with his shoulders dropped. She knew that body language all too well. He hovered close to the door, looking like he wanted to bolt. She took the envelope and stuffed it into her purse quickly, nodded, and left.

ANDREW NEIDERMAN

Allan stopped holding his breath and then turned to Joe, who stood there gently shaking his head.

"I almost hope for her sake that there's nothing there," he said.

For Allan, he could have said nothing more damaging to their relationship.

Joe saw it immediately in Allan's face.

"Almost," he added. "Of course, like you, I'd love to be part of some significant step forward."

Allan nodded.

"This might be more than a step, Joe. It could be a leap."

Joe nodded.

"She's very nice," he said, nodding at the door through which Demi had just left.

"Yes. Too nice for the man she has."

"Oh?" Joe smiled. "Do I detect more than scientific interest in your voice?"

"Forget it. I'm here only for the research," Allan said, and Joe laughed.

"Convince yourself, not me," he told him.

Frankie heard what Dr. Reuben was saying, but it was as if he had left his own body and was standing off to the side listening to the conversation between his body and his doctor. It occurred to him that this was like moving through the streets knowing you were in the sights of some hit man's high-powered rifle. Whenever he had the whim or desire, he would simply press his finger down on the trigger, and your head would explode. The bastards who had put the hit on you wanted the tension and anticipation to linger for as long as possible so you would suffer. Instead of your doctor, someone delivered a simple message that read, "You're a target. Any day. Any moment. There's no place to hide."

Maybe, then, it was better never to go to a doctor, never to hear any possible bad news.

"I'd like to start chemotherapy immediately, Mr. Vico. Doctor Weber will handle your treatments. He's an excellent oncologist."

"What are my chances here?"

"Why don't we wait to see what . . ."

"Give it to me straight, Doc," Frankie ordered. "I never pussy around. I don't want anyone to pussy around with me—lawyers, doctors, whatever."

"About thirty percent of patients with second stage lung cancer survive five years," Dr. Reuben said, almost taking pleasure in the abrupt response Frankie demanded.

"So it could be less?" Frankie asked. He wouldn't tolerate false hope or any sugarcoating. Dr. Reuben nodded.

"It could be. I'd like to admit you this afternoon."

Frankie looked out the window. The first thought that came to his mind was he might not be around for Chipper's graduation from law school.

"Let's see if we can slow this thing down, Mr. Vico. There are all sorts of breakthroughs happening as well, and no one can predict what weapons we might have in a year. It's better to go at this with some hope."

"Yeah, I getcha," Frankie said. "Okay. I'll make arrangements to check in."

"See if you can manage to be there by three," Dr. Reuben said. "I'll start what I have to in order to get you going."

"Right," Frankie said.

Dr. Reuben smiled and walked away.

What's he smiling for? Frankie thought and for the first time wondered if his doctor not only didn't care about him, but was happy to see him dying. Just like he didn't like some of his customers and couldn't care less if a piano fell on their heads, his doctor probably saw this as some sort of poetic justice countering the stupid saying about the good dying young. Maybe he wouldn't work too hard on saving or prolonging his life. Frankie made a mental note to have a second doctor evaluate and report about everything that was done.

If he shortchanges me, I'll be the last one he does, Frankie vowed. It felt a great deal better to be angry and think violent thoughts. He despised people who bathed in self-pity, and he was never a whiner.

"How'd it go?" Tony asked when he came out to the car.

"You didn't smoke in the fucking car, did you?" Frankie responded.

"No, boss."

"It went lousy. I gotta go the hospital. Get me back to the bowling alley," he ordered and got into the car.

Tony moved quickly.

"What's it about?" he asked as he started the engine.

"It's about dying, schmuck. Just drive. I got some figuring to do."

"Right," Tony said. He bit down on his lower lip almost as if he was afraid something stupid would come out of his mouth and Frankie would shoot him in the head just to shut him up.

When they arrived at the bowling alley, Frankie went right to Marilyn. She seemed incapable of understanding anything but the fact that she had to get things together for him and accompany him to the hospital.

"You don't really have cancer," she said, grimacing, as if he had made the choice to have it, as if it was entirely his own fault.

"Naw. It's just in everyone's imagination," Frankie said. "What? You think I'm checking into a hospital for kicks? Jesus, Marilyn. It ain't the Ritz."

She shook her head and moved as if she was humoring him. It wasn't until he was checked in, dressed in a hospital gown, and in the hospital bed in a private room with bedpans and IV stands nearby that she actually looked like she believed it.

"Everyone looks smaller in a hospital gown," she commented when he got into the bed.

He opened and closed his fists as if he were squeezing some invisible rubber ball.

"Thanks. I love hearing it. Just stay on top of things while I'm in here," he told her. "Watch that bartender. He looks like the type who steals nickels and dimes."

"Then why'd you hire him?"

"It was a favor for someone, Marilyn. I told you that."

"Okay," she said.

"Call Chipper. Let him know what's up."

"You sure you don't want to do it yourself? I hate telling people bad things."

"Chipper's not people, Marilyn. He's my son. Just do it," he said, not wanting to admit that he didn't want to tell his son himself. His son still thought he was invulnerable, a powerful man who made other men tremble just by looking in their direction. In a world where the rich and powerful ruled the roost, it was suicidal to admit to any weaknesses, much less fatal illnesses. Once it got out, the creeps would be coming out of their holes to challenge everything.

Dr. Reuben came in with Joe Weber.

"You better go," Frankie told Marilyn. "I'll talk to you later. Don't forget to call Chipper."

"Okay," she said, grateful for the reprieve. She kissed him, smiled at the doctors, and left.

Joe began to describe the protocol. Halfway through, Frankie interrupted to ask if there were other cancer patients on the same floor. Both doctors looked confused by the question.

"Well, there's someone next door being treated for lung cancer as well, Mr. Vico. He's one of my patients. Why do you ask?"

"It felt like I wasn't alone with this. Felt like it was a segregated wing of the hospital or something. I don't like feeling I'm in some graveyard already."

"That's not the case. There are patients here with different diagnoses," Joe told him.

"Yeah, well, okay. Keep talking," Frankie said. "I'm all ears."

Afterward, since he was about an hour or so from the beginning of his first treatment, Frankie got out of bed and took a walk. He was curious about the patient with lung cancer next door and peered through the open doorway. He saw on the door that his name was Paul Wellman.

Ain't that an ironic name, he thought.

Paul Wellman didn't look much more than forty. He was coughing and spitting into a handkerchief. A fairly attractive blonde sat watching him. Frankie imagined she was his wife. There's a thing, he thought, watching your husband die. She's probably planning the funeral. And suddenly, he hated all the bereaved. They ain't cryin' because they're sad, he thought. They're cryin' out of happiness that it's not them. The bastards.

"How's he doin'?" he asked when the woman turned toward the doorway and saw him standing there. Wellman looked his way, too, but not with any real interest.

"I'm next door," he said.

"Oh." She gave him a weak smile. "He's doing just fine," she said. "Fine. He'll be fine."

"Good," he muttered and walked on. Stupid broad was already in another world, he thought. Marilyn, on the other hand, isn't even going to skip a meal.

Allan had an unorthodox idea, but one that might give a quicker result. When he mentioned it to Joe, Joe balked.

"We can't do that, Allan."

"Why not?"

"C'mon, you know all this as well as I do. First, it might give the patient and his family false hope. And even if you saw some similar recuperation, you couldn't be sure of the reason, not without the findings. Besides, I don't have anyone who's gone beyond the point of traditional treatments yet, and no other doctor is going to agree to this. I've never had a patient try anything in the experimental stage."

"Precisely my point."

"But we can't claim that was the purpose for the transfusion, Allan. I didn't give her the transfusion as a miracle cure or tell her parents there was even that possibility."

"Hey, you have to step out of the box with this thing, Joe. It doesn't respect proper procedures, ethical acts. It's like being in a war with someone who's never signed the Geneva convention."

"It's a disease, Allan. It's not an enemy army," Joe said. "Let's take it a step at a time. I'm right beside you all the way, if we do this correctly."

Allan nodded but thought, He doesn't get it. We've got to replicate what they did with the mice. A cancer-free mouse passed on its miraculous white blood cells to its progeny. Those cells were used to fight cancers in normal mice. If this kid has some special biological gift, it has to be transfused into another human being who happened to be suffering from a particularly virulent form of cancer. That's the way to do the research. Not spend weeks, months, analyzing the DNA. Furthermore, someone might be saved right here and now.

He regretted not simply taking Taylor Petersen's blood specimen back to L.A. where he was king.

Later, when Joe called him at the hospital to tell him where they were going for dinner, he opted out.

"I'll just have something here," he said. "I want to get some of this preliminary work done in the lab and get into the slides. You know I'll have to head back to Los Angeles for the rest of the work, Joe."

"You coming back to the house tonight though, right?"

"Sure. I'm in for another day if Toby doesn't mind."

"Of course, she doesn't mind."

Allan thanked him. He knew Joe's wife wasn't fond of him, but he could care less about friendships now. While he was in the lab, he went on the hospital computer and looked at the descriptions of the various patients. He paused when he read about Paul Wellman. Joe hadn't even mentioned this patient, a patient ideal for a last hope effort of any kind. But what made it more amazing was Wellman had O/Rh blood type.

He sat back and thought about it. Here was an opportunity. Why not go straight on in? Take a shot? Despite the unorthodoxy and violations of medical procedure, he'd be taking quite a risk in another sense. If there was a reason why this didn't work on Wellman, he would have lost his sample, and returning to the Petersens for more of the kid's blood this soon might really spook Demi Petersen. There was also the very issue of how much would be needed to have an effect. Maybe this wasn't enough. It was more prudent to do the research, break down the DNA, follow all the protocols. If he didn't do it all right, no one would accept his findings anyway.

Why am I remaining here? he then thought. I should get back to my home turf.

He considered packing up the samples and leaving, but then he looked at the computer information again. All the time in between, all the steps to the research, all of the findings would take so long. It ate away at him. He pondered and teased himself with the possibilities. Later, he did try to eat some dinner, but he was such a bundle of nervous energy, he barely ate anything.

He returned to the lab and looked at some of the preliminary information on the first tube of blood specimens. The kid's numbers were terrific, especially his chemistry, but there was nothing that indicated anything unusual. As he pondered, his cell phone buzzed, and he picked up his call. It was Thornton Carver.

"Sorry to tell you, Allan. We lost Zoe Livingston. She put up quite a fight for a twelve-year-old."

Allan didn't speak.

"How is it going there? Anything worthwhile?"

"I'm not sure, Thornton. I might remain another day or so."

"Hey, take your time. You have yet to take a vacation."

"Cancer doesn't, so I don't," he replied dryly.

Thornton grunted rather than laughed.

"Watch yourself, Allan. You're burning out at this high speed."

Allan finally laughed and then told Thornton about his nearly getting a very serious speeding ticket.

"Well, you see? We have some perks after all," Thornton Carver said. "Call me."

"Will do," Allan said.

After he ended the call, he sat back and closed his eyes. He vividly recalled Zoe Livingston from the first day she was admitted to the hospital. He could see her faith in him, her hope when he spoke to and treated her, and the optimism he had planted in her parents. He now felt like a total fraud. He was helpless, after all—Superman without anything but the costume. The disease was doing this to him, playing with him, tormenting and torturing him. In his mind, perhaps close to some state of madness, Cancer was a living monster, a creature that walked the earth and toyed with fools like him who believed they were any competition whatsoever.

His all too familiar rage roared inside him and tired him out. He closed his eyes again, and this time, his fatigue took a firm grasp and sent him spiraling deep into sleep. When he woke, he was surprised to find himself still in the same chair. He checked the time and realized it was close to one in the morning. It also surprised him that Joe hadn't called. He checked his phone to be sure. There were no messages. Maybe he was hoping I returned to Los Angeles, he thought. He scrubbed his face with his dry palms and then looked at the blinking computer screen.

Paul Wellman's chart was still up.

He stared at it and then stood up and looked around the quiet lab.

"It's all a crapshoot anyway," he practically screamed at the equipment.

Still reeling from his rage, he scooped up the white blood cells he had separated from Taylor Petersen's blood samples and marched out with everything else he needed. No one paid him much attention. He went to the elevator and stepped out on Paul Wellman's floor. For a split second, he hesitated and tried to change his mind, but he was driven by something greater than himself now. He was Captain Ahab. He was on the verge of facing Moby Dick.

He went directly to Wellman's room.

Frankie Vico had undergone his first chemotherapy treatment. He had lain there waiting for it to hit him like a punch in the stomach. He had some indigestion, a dryness in his mouth, and the beginning of a real killer of a headache, but the dramatic side effects were waiting to pounce, probably with the next treatment. They had done too good of a job preparing him for what to expect. Just listening to it all was pure torture. Now, he found he couldn't sleep. He was restless and so anxious he felt like screaming.

Almost in a rage, he threw off his blanket and sat up. Why was this happening to him? What the hell was going on? If the Big Boss wanted him gone, why didn't he just have him in a head-on crash or marked for a hit and get it done? Of course, perhaps He was enjoying torturing him.

Christ, he had started this health kick, hadn't he? Look at how good he looked these days. This made no sense. Maybe something the doctor had told him to do led to this situation. None of them seemed to know what the hell they were doing. They weren't even good at investing their money.

He scooped up his robe, slipped into it and his slippers, and went for a damn walk. Maybe it would be his last. When he stepped into the hallway, he looked toward the nurse's station. There were only two, and they were so involved in their conversation they weren't even paying attention to monitors, much less able to see him wandering about. He wondered if the poor bastard next door was still alive. Maybe he died hours ago and no one knew, not that it mattered. Nothing mattered anymore.

Practically skating over the tiled floor, he made his way up to Paul Wellman's door and looked in at him. Despite the late hour, his doctor appeared to be there. Wellman looked unconscious. The doctor had his back to the door and was apparently injecting something into Wellman's arm. He watched as the doctor made some quick moves while keeping the needle in Wellman's arm. Finally, he was finished and stepped back. He just stood there looking down at Wellman for a while before turning to leave. He stopped dead in his tracks when he saw Frankie in the doorway.

Frankie was surprised it was not Dr. Weber.

"Can I help you?" the doctor asked.

"I'm next door. Just looking in on him. What's happening?"

"He's resting comfortably," he said. "You shouldn't disturb him now."

"Who's disturbing him?"

Frankie stepped back as the doctor rushed toward him. He moved quickly out of the room and away. Frankie watched him hurry down to the elevator and push the button. He looked back once. Weird, Frankie thought, glanced in at Wellman, and then continued his walk, thinking, Dead Man Walking. He wanted to chant it in fact.

Allan Parker stepped into the elevator and stood there looking at him until the door closed.

"Fucking doctors," Frankie muttered. He walked on and then got so tired he wasn't sure he'd make it back. In fact, he had to stop and lean against the wall to get his balance. One of the nurses finally saw him and came to him quickly.

"Mr. Vico. What are you doing out here?"

"Looking for a pizza," he said.

She smiled and shook her head. "Let's go back to your room," she said, taking his arm.

"You're going back with me? I don't know as I'm up to it, although I'll give it the old college try."

"I'm taking *you* back," she said sharply. "To rest. You need your rest."

"Yeah, yeah. Say, what does this chemo crap do to your sex drive?"

"Save your questions for your doctor, Mr. Vico."

He paused at Wellman's door again.

"There was another doctor just here," he told the nurse. "Kinda late for him, ain't it? Is he about to kick the bucket or what?"

"Another doctor?" She smiled and shook her head. "I don't think so, Mr. Vico."

"I saw him. I spoke to him!" he emphasized.

She simply held her smile as if she were talking to a

complete idiot. "I assure you that I would know, Mr. Vico."

"Well, someone was here. Someone gave him an injection or something."

She stopped smiling.

"When?"

"Ten minutes ago if that," he said. "I watched him doing it. He wasn't the nicest guy on the block either."

"Let's get you back to bed," she told him.

"Don't believe me. You can't ask him," he said nodding at Wellman. "He didn't wake up even though the guy was sticking him. Maybe he's already dead. Hey, wait a minute," he said, forcefully stopping himself and the nurse. He looked back at the elevator as if there was some significant evidence he might have missed.

"Now what, Mr. Vico?" the nurse asked.

"Maybe someone came up here and took him out of his misery. Ever think of that, Nurse . . ." He looked at her tag. "Dakota?"

Her face grew more serious now.

"You're named after a state?" he asked.

"You didn't really see anyone up here just now, did you, Mr. Vico?"

"He was in there. I spoke to him. He told me not to disturb Wellman and then he walked out quickly. He practically ran, come to think of it, and went to the elevator."

"Come along," she said with more urgency.

She took him to his bed and helped him get comfortable.

"Maybe Wellman's wife sent someone up. Get it?" he asked the nurse. "In his case, it ain't even a crime. It's a favor, ain't it? Huh?" he pursued.

"We don't practice euthanasia here, Mr. Vico. This is a place where we work at getting people better, cured."

"Right. Cure me, will ya."

"I'm sure your doctor is trying," she replied and walked out quickly.

Moments later, he heard another pair of footsteps and saw both nurses pass his door. He was still restless, despite his fatigue. He listened and heard more coming and going, but he didn't have the strength to get himself up again. He needed some rest. The nurse had been right about that. Hospitals, however, were famous as places where people could get no rest. You had to be unconscious.

He fell asleep, finally, and was woken in the morning by loud chatter and even some laughter in the hallway. Curiosity gave him the energy and strength to sit up and then get out of his bed. He shoved his feet into his slippers and this time was so curious he didn't bother going first for his robe. They could see his rear end. He didn't care. He went to the door and looked out. The morning nursing shift had arrived, and all the nurses were talking to Nurse Dakota and the other nurse who had been with her. They were on their way out. Everyone was standing in front of Wellman's door.

"What's going on?" he demanded.

They all turned to look at him, but no one spoke for a moment. Then Nurse Dakota approached him.

"You told me last night you saw a doctor here."

"So?"

"See?" she said to the others.

They looked at him as if he had seen a ghost or something.

"What the hell's going on?" he demanded, more intently this time.

Before any of them could respond, Paul Wellman stepped out of his room. He was in his robe and slippers, and he was smiling.

"When's breakfast?" he asked.

They all stared at him.

"Hey!" Frankie called to him.

Wellman looked at him.

"Ain't you supposed to be dying?"

Wellman smiled and nodded. "Shows you," he said without coughing, "you can't believe one half of what you read and three quarters of what you hear."

"What about what you see?"

"At least ten percent. Maybe, in my case, ninety," he joked.

"Where's your wife?"

"She's on her way with something decent to eat," Wellman told him.

Everyone turned when the elevator opened and Joe Weber came hurrying out.

"Uh-oh," Wellman said. "Here comes my doctor. I better behave myself and stop chasing the nurses."

Frankie saw the look of amazement on Dr. Weber's face as he approached.

Nurse Dakota stepped closer to Frankie.

ANDREW NEIDERMAN

"Could it be that Doctor Weber was the doctor you saw last night?" she asked in a whisper.

"No."

"Are you sure?"

"He's my doctor, too, ain't he? I think I would recognize him."

She nodded.

"But I can tell you this, Nurse Dakota."

"What?"

"Whoever the hell he was, I want him coming to see me today," he replied.

CHAPTER FOUR

There was a room with a cot reserved for anyone working very late hours in the laboratory. When Joe stepped into the laboratory, all the technicians turned toward him. It was as if he had brought a rough, chilling wind along. He panned the room and then approached Shirley Cavner, who had some blood slides under a microscope.

"I'm looking for Doctor Parker, an associate of mine. We were in here yester—"

"He's taking a nap, Doctor. Or shall I say, 'still sleeping.' He was in there when I arrived this morning, and he hasn't come out yet," she replied, nodding at the door of the side room. Joe nodded and approached the room.

Allan was asleep with his back to the door. Joe stood there looking in on him a moment and then looked back. The technicians were still watching him, but when he looked at them, they all returned to their work.

He nudged Allan, who groaned and turned slowly.

"Did you do something with Paul Wellman last night, Allan?" Joe asked, not hiding his boiling rage. "Did you?"

Allan scrubbed his eyes with his closed fists a moment and then sat up.

"What is it?" he asked.

"I asked about Paul Wellman, Allan. Did you do something? Well?"

"What's happened?"

"Allan, just tell me the truth!"

"I gambled," he confessed.

"You gambled. This isn't Las Vegas, Allan! Don't you realize that you could have created a serious lawsuit for me and for the hospital?"

"Why? What damage can you do to a man who's dying anyway, Joe? There's nothing more you can do for him. You know it. Is he gone?"

Weber looked away.

"Joe? Did he pass away?"

Joe's continued silence sent a chilling, electric shot through Allan. It nearly lifted him off the cot.

"Joe?"

Weber continued to look away, but his silence spoke mouthfuls.

"He's in remission, isn't he? Jesus, man, what's going on?"

"I can't come to any conclusions yet. I have him being scanned as we speak," he said.

"Why? Why, Joe?" Allan pursued.

"He shocked the nurses this morning. He was up and about asking about breakfast. His vitals are nearly perfect and he's not coughing at all. His lungs . . ."

"What?"

"Sound clear."

Allan fell back on the cot, looking like he had been hit by a sledgehammer.

"Wow," he cried, and punched his left palm. "I knew it. I knew it my very soul."

"Regardless of any of this, you did a terrible thing, Allan."

"Saving his life?"

"You know what I mean. Protocol. You know I could be in deep shit permitting you to go at my patient."

"Forget all that," Allan said. "I've been sick of the politics in medicine from the day I started, kissing ass to get funding, meeting with the most obnoxious, self-serving politicians, dealing with hospital bureaucrats with swollen egos. They know little about what we are doing and yet have all this power over us."

"It's the system we're in, Allan."

"You're in. I've never accepted it."

Joe folded his arms across his chest and stood straighter.

"Can you tell me how I'm going to explain this without revealing all these breaches in protocol? You've established a list of violations an arm and a leg long. Besides, to do it, we'll have to reveal the kid, and then what? We could have done all this correctly, intelligently, protecting the findings."

"Don't say anything to anyone yet," Allan told him, quickly interrupting. "Let's confirm the results first. C'mon. We have so much to do."

Weber looked at him. "It might be better if you just leave, Allan. I'll call you."

"What? No way. Don't be a fool. You could make some mistake here and send us reeling back to the Dark Ages, because that's where we are."

"Not quite."

"We were for my mother, and we were for that little girl you released yesterday, Joe, and I was treating a girl about her age who died yesterday."

Weber blinked and then shook his head. "I don't like this. I don't mind telling you. I'm terrified, Allan."

"Don't be. Months, maybe even weeks from now, you'll be considered a medical hero. Look," he added when Joe didn't move, "if what I did with Wellman comes out, I'll accept all the blame here. I'll admit to doing anything and everything without your knowledge. You called me in as a consultant, and I went haywire. You won't be blamed. I'll put it in writing, whatever you want. Do you want me to speak to someone right now?"

"No," Joe quickly replied. "Not yet," he added. "We haven't confirmed anything, and no one really knows anything."

"Okay, then, we're fine."

"Fine," Joe repeated smirking.

"Let's follow up on Wellman and take this a step at a time, Joe."

"Is it all gone, the entire blood sample?"

Allan nodded.

"I didn't know what dosage to apply, obviously, so I thought I would give him the whole thing. It was an all-or-nothing shot."

"Even though he was terminal, you were taking that shot with another human being's life, Allan."

"We do it everyday, Joe. Stop sugarcoating. Every desperate physician out there with a terminal patient is throwing the dice with this protocol or that in hopes of a Las Vegas–style win. I did nothing different."

Joe nodded and then softened his face.

"Toby thinks you might be a vampire. This will surely confirm it."

"I'd be anything to win this war," Allan replied.

"I don't doubt it."

They started out. All the technicians stopped to watch them leave.

It was in the air.

Something unusual was going on.

It carried over to radiology. Morton Feinberg stared incredulously at the pictures. He looked at Joe and Allan and then at the pictures scanned of Paul Wellman's lungs.

"They're gone," he said. He had said it about twenty times to himself. "All the tumors are gone. This guy has clean lungs. What's the story here? Look at his results from last week," he continued and turned them to Wellman's pictures where the tumors were clearly visible and invasive. "We're talking maybe six days?"

"It's clearly a miracle," Allan said. He looked at Joe, who was obviously at a loss for how to explain it without revealing Taylor. "I've been in the battle against cancer for years now, but I've never seen anything like it. We'll have to review everything that was done to see about combinations of treatments and the like, don't you think, Doctor Weber?"

"What? Oh, yes."

"For now," Allan said, "let's not make too much of this, Doctor Feinberg. There are cases of spontaneous remissions, but no one to date has provided a logical explanation for them. You know what could happen. Desperate people calling Doctor Weber here expecting similar results and here we don't know yet why."

Feinberg shrugged.

"It's your patient. Handle it whatever way you wish. Don't worry about me. Whoever I told this to would think I had lost it anyway. I'm not that brave."

"Very smart," Allan said. "We feel the same way, Doctor Feinberg. Joe?"

"Thanks, Morton. We'll redo these tests shortly, of course, to reconfirm."

"I'm here for you," Feinberg said. He actually looked a little terrified.

Allan smiled to himself. Perfect, he thought. He will keep his mouth shut.

"Let's go to my office," Joe said.

His offices were right across the street from the hospital, and he had no office hours until the following day. Neither of them spoke during their walk. Allan was far too excited, and Joe Weber couldn't throw off his sense of foreboding. Why, he wondered, wasn't he as ecstatic as Allan obviously was?

As soon as he closed his private office door behind him, he spun on Allan.

"You were exactly right with Morton. We don't even know exactly how to explain the phenomenon, Allan, so if I were you, I wouldn't think of rushing to make any sort of announcement."

"Of course not," Allan said.

Joe looked at him skeptically and then sat behind his desk. Allan sat on the light-brown leather sofa.

"You're going to have to figure out a way to get the boy to give you another, perhaps more significant, sample and then start on a correct protocol for this. Take it back to Thornton Carver and get a real study begun. No more experiments on actual patients," he emphasized. "I won't be party to any. I mean it, Allan."

"Absolutely. You're absolutely right."

"If you offer them money again, I wouldn't offer them too much more. It will trigger anxiety. Maybe . . . tell them the samples were . . ."

"Contaminated? Perfect. Good thinking, Joe. They'll buy that. I'll be very convincing, pretend to be the arrogant big-city doctor and blame the boondock laboratory here, blame myself for not rushing off to Los Angeles, and offer them . . . fifteen hundred this time. How's that?"

"They'll buy the arrogant big-city doctor part," Joe said dryly.

"Very funny. You know what?" he continued before Weber could say anything else. "That's what we're going to do anyway. I'll head back to L.A. You won't have to be involved in this at all after that."

For a split second, Joe's ego flared. Allan Parker could

win the Nobel Prize or something, and he would not even be a footnote.

"I'm not saying I don't want to be involved. If Wellman's results hold up, I'm sure he's not going to be complaining to any medical boards about me. Wellman certainly didn't know what was happening."

Allan smiled.

"Now you're thinking sensibly. Of course, you're going to be cited as part of this, Joe. You had the foresight to put me on the right track. If you hadn't called me to begin with, where would I be with it? You had the insight, the right perception, and instincts."

"I mean, none of that is as important as our doing this correctly now, so the findings are accepted, that is," Joe said. "I'm not trying to stroke my own ego."

"You don't have to explain any of that to me, Joe. I'm the one submerged in the damn cesspool of medical politics regarding cancer research. There'll be lots of envious bastards out there either trying to hop on the bandwagon or knock us off. The concept of pure science is just that, a concept, not a reality. There's no room for fumbling the ball."

Joe nodded and looked at him. Then he smiled.

"Jesus Christ, Allan. I think this is really it."

"I know," Allan replied.

Finally, the two congratulated each other, pumping a handshake and beaming like two college buddies high on life and their futures.

While across the street, Paul Wellman sat up in his bed and greeted his wife and friends, who literally had been planning his funeral. The festive atmosphere spilled out of the room and down the hallway to the nurses' station.

Happiness, like tragedy and sadness, was contagious, especially in a hospital so eager to welcome smiles and laughter.

"You got to be kiddin' me," Jim Fields said, as he finished pouring his beer into his glass.

Jim was the most finicky, neatest man Warren knew. He hated drinking out of a bottle. Even on a job site, he'd have a paper cup. His fellow construction workers nicknamed him Gentleman Jim. When he wasn't working, he always wore a light-blue tie with his dark-blue shirt and a clean pair of jeans. His hair was trim, and he was never out in public without being clean shaven, reeking of some sweet aftershave.

He turned on his stool at the Station House bar to look at Warren, who looked like he had throat muscles strong enough to suck the neck off the bottle.

Warren wiped his lips with the back of his hand and shook his head.

"Swear to God," he said. "One thousand bucks."

"Shit, man. I'd a done it for a hundred. That's a lot of money for somethin' like that, Warren. What's up with that?"

"This guy was weird," Warren said. "He looked . . . like he was high on something."

"Yeah, well, I heard doctors do that. After all, they can get to any drug they want. Where's this guy work?"

"That's another thing," Warren said. "He don't work in the desert. He's from Los Angeles."

"No shit?" Jim sipped some more of his beer and thought. "Something don't sound right is what I mean. So Taylor's cousin needs his blood. He gives it, and she's better today?"

"She's in school today. Demi won't say it, but Ralph was choosing a coffin."

"No shit?" Jim said. It was closing on becoming a chant. "Somethin' don't sound normal, Warren. A thousand dollars. Man, I'd look into that some more. Hey, if you see this doctor again, tell him you know someone who'd give twice as much blood for five hundred."

"You said a hundred before."

"Yeah, but somethin' don't sound normal." Jim sipped his beer. "Maybe you should ask somebody."

"Huh? Who?"

"Another doctor."

"I don't know any doctors. I ain't been to a doctor in twenty years."

"No shit?"

"That's the truth. I take care of myself. I don't even carry health insurance. I wish I knew more about this whole thing though."

Jim shrugged. "You could maybe talk to Doctor Edwards?"

"That workman's compensation quack?"

"He's still a doctor."

Warren thought, sucked some more beer. "He'd probably charge something."

"Might be worth it," Jim said. "Somethin' don't sound normal. If this doctor comes around again, and you want to negotiate, it'd be better if you knew somethin' intelligent to say, don'tcha think?"

"Yeah, I suppose so."

"Say, I just remembered that Basil Cotter's going to see him this afternoon at two 'bout his leg. Needs another month of checks. You could go along with him and maybe start a conversation. Basil won't care."

Warren nodded. "Yeah, maybe."

"Not like you got somethin' else important to do," Jim said, smiling. "Like I said, maybe you'll learn somethin' that'll get you more moola out of this doctor from Los Angeles if he comes callin' again."

"Yeah, maybe," Warren said. He nodded. "Something is definitely not normal."

"Absolutely," Jim said. He adjusted his tie and brushed down his shirt. "Give Basil a call. He's home workin' on his limp. I swear he oughta be in show business."

"What else do you think this all is, if not show business?" Warren quipped, gesturing to indicate the world.

Jim smiled. "I hear ya," he said. He finished his beer. "I hear you real good."

Warren thought a little more and then got Basil Cotter's phone number from Jim. Two hours later, he picked him up at his apartment complex and drove him to Indio where Dr. Gordon Edwards had his office above a small motel.

Gordon Edwards had not started with the intention of becoming a half-assed physician, but early on in his career he was caught in three serious malpractice cases, one following the other too soon for the insurance companies. His premiums skyrocketed, and the medical office rent choked him. He couldn't find a doctor willing to take him in as a partner and retreated to the medical life and career he now enjoyed. He didn't consider himself incompetent or mediocre by any means. He thought of himself as unlucky and abused by the system. Consequently, he actually took pleasure in screwing insurance companies and government agencies. Every phony prescription he wrote and every false diagnosis he made gave him a sense of revenge. There was no other explanation for him continuing what he was doing. Medicine had long since lost its excitement. He was only in his early forties and seriously considering going into law. "If you can't beat them, join them" should have been written across his forehead, he thought.

He was a little suspicious of Warren Moore accompanying Basil Cotter. He didn't like his patients, if he could still call them that, presenting him with possible witnesses. Just to be sure, he gave Basil as close to a legitimate examination as possible. As Gordon was writing up his findings, Warren began with, "I've got a weird situation involving a doctor from Los Angeles."

Gordon looked up. His thoughts were written across his face: so that was it. Warren was looking for an expert witness in some lawsuit.

"I don't testify against other doctors, no matter what I'm offered," he said.

"I ain't talking about court or anything like that," Warren said. He looked indignant.

"Oh. Well . . ." Gordon checked his watch to clearly indicate he was finished, but Warren went right into the events concerning Taylor, and when he mentioned the thousand-dollar payment, Gordon sat back.

"A thousand dollars? Just for no more than a normal blood screening?"

"That's it, Doc."

"Describe that little girl's problem again."

"I don't know how to describe it. She had some cancer, leukemia or something. She was dying is all I was told. Maybe it was bullshit, but everyone in the family took it very seriously, and the only time I saw her, she looked sickly to me."

Gordon shook his head.

"Something doesn't sound right, Mr. Moore. I couldn't possibly explain anything or give you any advice without more information about the girl herself."

"Well, why would he pay the kid a thousand bucks? As I said, he didn't take that much blood. What are they paying for a pint these days, for chrissakes?"

"Nowhere near a thousand bucks. I can tell you that. Look, it's not my field of expertise, Mr. Moore, but if I were to conjecture—"

"Huh?"

"Take a guess. I would surmise that there's some research project, well-funded, and they're doing work on DNA or something. Obviously, something has excited them about your girlfriend's son's blood. I have no idea what that could be."

"So, they don't offer just anyone this kind of money?"

"I wouldn't think so. Not for just that. People get paid good money to be part of a test group, but this doesn't sound at all like that. Why don't you just ask the doctor?"

"He's probably gone, and I don't trust him. Something ain't right about him."

"Well . . . no one's the worse for anything, and your girlfriend's son is a thousand dollars richer. Whether it had anything to do with the little girl's recovery is something only the researchers will determine."

Warren nodded. He wasn't learning anything much he could use.

"What if that doctor comes back for more blood?"

"That would probably mean there was something further to explore."

"What?" He almost added "damn it" out of frustration.

"Something obviously to do with the immune system or tumor reduction, I'd surmise."

"A cure for cancer?"

"I doubt that," Gordon said, smiling. "Not just from his blood. But something that might some day lead to a cure perhaps. Medical research is a big business these days. Then again, what isn't?" he asked, mostly for himself.

"So, maybe we should ask for more money?"

"I couldn't say," Gordon said. "Well . . . it never hurts to ask though, does it?" He smiled.

"No," Warren said. "Thanks."

"What the hell was that all about?" Basil asked him on the way back to Palm Springs.

"I'm not sure, but I might just find out soon," Warren told him.

Basil thanked him for giving him a lift. Almost before the words were out of his mouth, Warren shot off.

"Crazy bastard," Basil muttered, looked at the paper that would get him his workman's compensation, and put the rest of it out of his mind.

CHAPTER FIVE

Demi's heart began to race when she saw Allan Parker step out of his automobile the moment she emerged from the beauty salon. She liked him well enough, but she had hoped, selfishly perhaps, that there wouldn't be anymore direct contact with him and the research. Playing around with her son's blood and health made her nervous enough without all the other possible ramifications afterward. Something wonderful had occurred. Jodi was okay. Taylor was part of it for a short while and that would be that. Nothing else would complicate their lives.

She looked around as if searching for an avenue of escape. It was drawing close to the daylight saving time change, and she knew that it wouldn't be long before she would leave work at twilight—especially because they were so close to the San Jacinto Mountain range, which seemed to grow taller and taller to bring down the sun earlier and earlier this time of the year.

The traffic on Palm Canyon Boulevard was brisk. It was still a great time of the year to be in the desert, and visitors were flowing in to enjoy the weather at discount prices.

"Hello, Mrs. Petersen," Allan said, approaching her. "Do you need a ride home by any chance?"

"No, thank you. I have my own car," she said.

Allan nodded and stood there smiling at her.

"Anything wrong?" she asked.

Now that he was here facing her, being in any way deceitful seemed impossible. Surely, he didn't have to find ways to manipulate her. She was too nice, too trusting, and too loving. It made him uncomfortable to think about doing it, and besides, he wasn't very good at deception. Just like he appreciated clarity in his work, he appreciated it in people, too.

Besides, the fabrication about the blood being corrupted had major disadvantages. It would be unwise to give her the impression the laboratory was incompetent. It could influence her opinion about anything he told her afterward as well.

"Nothing's wrong, Mrs. Petersen. Something, however, is quite right."

"What?"

"Can we get a cup of coffee or something? I would like to talk to you."

"Why?"

"This is big, Mrs. Petersen, bigger than both of us," he said.

She considered him, and for a moment, he thought she would simply take up his invitation, but his obvious excitement also had spooked her a little. It was just so hard for him to be so patient.

"Let's go to my home," she said.

Demi knew Warren would be there, and her instincts were telling her to have a witness, another pair of ears and eyes, and, most important, someone with whom to confer. She believed that despite his obvious failings, Warren was a rock. She was with him because she sensed his strength. He made her feel safe. It was like going through life with her own personal bodyguard, not only to protect her against creeps in the streets, but creeps in suits and ties. Didn't he return with her to the auto dealership last year and get the salesman to reduce the price of the car she wanted, and considerably, too? There were just too many places where a woman alone was still vulnerable in this society.

Besides, Allan Parker made her very nervous stalking her like this. Why didn't he just call before he came? How long had he been waiting out here? Why didn't he come into the salon? She never knew a doctor to behave this way.

"Sure," Allan said. "I'll follow you."

She flicked a smile and hurried to her car. He stood watching her as if he didn't believe she had one of her own. When she started it, he got into his and pulled out behind her. She fumbled for her cell phone. Warren better be there, she thought. He answered on the third ring.

"Doctor Parker is following me home. He was waiting for me outside of the beauty salon," she began as soon as he said, "Hello."

"Oh, yeah? Why?"

"He wants to talk to me. I think it's about Taylor's blood sample."

Warren was quiet.

"Warren?"

"What did you tell him?"

"Nothing yet. I didn't let him say anything. He wanted to take me for coffee."

"You did the right thing. He either wants his money back or wants more of Taylor's blood," he said. "He's not getting either so easily."

"I don't think he wants his money back, Warren."

"Um. We'll see."

"We'll be there in ten minutes. Is Taylor in his room?"

"Where else would he be? I bet he's surfing the Internet for porn."

"Stop it, Warren."

"Hey, I hope he is. At least we'll know he's a little normal."

"He's only fifteen, Warren. I know it's easy to forget but . . ."

"I lost my virginity at thirteen, and kids today are supposed to be even wilder when it comes to that stuff. Taylor's not what you call a normal teenager, Demi," he told her. "Forget it. Just get home."

She was so nervous she almost missed a turn to her own house. When she pulled into the driveway, Warren's car blocked her entrance to the garage as usual. Allan had to park on the street. He did so quickly and hurried to join her at the front door as if he thought she might go in and lock him out. The thought had actually occurred to her, but Warren pulled the door open before she could reach for the handle. He stood looking out at the two of them and smiled.

He was dressed in a faded blue athletic T-shirt, which revealed his sharply cut muscular arms and shoulders, a pair of jeans, and was barefoot. He had a bottle of beer in his right hand, gripping it at the neck as if he wanted to use it as a club.

"Well, well, the good doctor again. And here I thought you guys didn't make house calls anymore," he said, widening his smile at what he thought was his own cleverness.

"This is very important, Mr. . . ." Allan realized he didn't remember his name. He was never significant enough for him to care.

"Moore," Warren said. "Like in, 'I want more.' Every time someone says that, I get a phone call," he added. It was his signature joke.

"Warren, please," Demi said. She looked like she would faint.

Warren backed away to let them enter, as Demi turned to Allan.

"Let's go in the living room," she said. He glanced at Warren, who was still smiling dumbly, and followed her.

Allan sensed this was not going to be easy. He would have to draw on all his people skills. He hoped he had the patience. He couldn't ever throw off the feeling that he was racing time, sprinting beside every clock. All over America, indeed the world, cancer patients were waiting anxiously to hear about his work, his discoveries. Like some ubiquitous Superman, he was everywhere fighting evil. His name was on every victim's lips. "Allan Parker will save us. Have no fear."

"Please," Demi said indicating the sofa.

She sat in the chair across from it. Warren remained standing. He was no longer smiling, and he put down his bottle of beer and folded his arms across his chest. His eyes grew small and intent as he assumed the demeanor of an Israeli Mossad agent anticipating some act of terror. He hovered closely, still wearing that wise-guy smile.

"Thank you," Allan said.

"So, what's this about, Doctor Parker?" Demi asked.

"Well, as you know," he began, offering his most successful bedside tone and smile, "we were fascinated by the wonderful reversal of your niece's critical stage right after she received Taylor's blood. You were kind enough to give us the sample."

"Taylor gave the sample," Demi corrected softly.

"We know all that. You paid for it. It was a done deal," Warren added sharply.

"Of course. Anyway, I began an analysis here and intended to go forward with my research in Los Angeles."

He hesitated, realizing he was about to reveal some serious medical procedural violations, but he was also confident that these people had no idea what was correct and what was not when it came to protocols and therapies.

"So?" Warren said. "Why are you back to see us? Why ain'tcha in Los Angeles?"

Allan didn't look at him.

"I lost a patient about the same age as your niece two days ago, Mrs. Petersen. It gets me crazy when children die from some form of cancer or another. In the minds of most people, cancer remains a disease striking mainly older folks. People are living longer, so their susceptibility to various cancers grows greater." Allan smiled. "Years ago, when people died at younger ages, there wasn't as much cancer. It didn't have a chance to strike because the body died before it could metastasize."

He glanced at Warren, whose forehead was creased. Allan could see he was getting confused and overwhelmed. The man's a simpleton, Allan thought, but he also warned himself not to say or do anything that would sound insulting or condescending. Like most ignoramuses, Warren had far more pride than justified. Ego appeared to grow in a direct correlation to stupidity.

Allan's stomach was buzzing with bees. He had so little patience for this sort of man, but he knew instinctively that he had better not even suggest it.

"Stop snowing us. What the hell do you want?" Warren asked, dropping his arms and stepping closer. "Your money back?"

"Oh, no. Quite the contrary." He looked at Demi to suggest she rein in Warren, but apparently she wasn't at all upset with her boyfriend. In fact, she looked happy that he was being so aggressive. It drained Allan's confidence.

"So what the hell is this?"

"I'm about to explain," Allan said calmly. "I was impatient," he continued, thinking he should admit to weakness and failings to show he was no different from them. "I didn't want to wait for all the research, testing, etc., so I went ahead and gave the white blood cells from Taylor's blood sample to another terminal cancer patient."

He paused. It suddenly occurred to him that he was

raising the value of Taylor's blood, doing, in effect, Warren Moore's work for him.

"And?" Warren asked.

"It appears to be helping," he said, couching his words as carefully as some merchant trader. "I think there just might be something significant to discover here."

Warren's head bobbed.

"Only you're out of Taylor's blood, is that it?" he asked, beaming.

"Yes."

"Figured," Warren said, looking to Demi.

No shit, Dick Tracy, Allan wanted very much to say, but stifled the very thought of doing so.

"You want more of Taylor's blood?" Demi asked quickly. She was afraid this was why he was coming to see them, but until this moment, she wouldn't permit herself to say it, even to herself.

"Another sample . . . maybe, a typical blood donation," Allan replied, trying desperately to sound nonchalant.

"Typical blood donation? You mean a pint?" Warren asked.

"I don't want to keep coming back here, and we do need enough to do the research now. My hope is we'll be able to duplicate the white blood cells and create . . ."

"A cure for cancer?" Demi finished for him, speaking in a little more than a whisper.

"Yes, exactly."

"I still don't understand why Taylor has this in his blood, this potential cure," she said.

"I don't know for sure, Mrs. Petersen, but as I previously

suggested, it might have something to do with the dosage of radiation your husband was exposed to before Taylor was born. If I were to offer a conjecture . . ."

"A what?" Warren asked, brightening on the word *offer*.

"A guess."

"Oh."

"Some genetic change occurred and was passed on to him."

"Because my husband never contacted any form of cancer even though he was exposed?"

"Well, I can't be sure your husband's natural genetic makeup was what was passed on to Taylor. Actually, there are a number of genetic formulas that might show us how this occurred, but that doesn't matter at this point. I don't want to get complicated and confuse you."

Warren grunted.

"Taylor's father had a heart attack," Warren said.

"That's a completely different set of circumstances, Mr. Moore."

Warren thought a moment, twitching his nose like a rabbit. "Could the kid get a heart attack?"

Demi froze with fear.

Allan smiled and shook his head. "Very unlikely. Nothing remotely indicates such an event."

"A pint, huh? What are you offering?" Warren asked, deciding it was time to cut to the chase.

Demi looked up at him. He gestured with the fingers of his left hand to indicate she should keep her mouth shut and remain still. Allan caught it.

"I can authorize . . . a payment of ten thousand dollars," he said.

Warren's eyes nearly exploded. Contrary to his reaction, however, Demi's reaction to such a jump in price for her son's blood sent a wave of terror through her body. She pressed her lips together and smothered a moan.

Warren grew more confident.

"To be completely honest, Doc, I spoke with a doctor today about what you've done already, so I ain't completely surprised at what you're saying or your being here," Warren said. "He thought the only possibility was that the kid has some miraculous DAN, NAD or something. Now, from what you're telling us, he could be the only one on the damn planet."

"I couldn't say," Allan said, even though he feared that might very well be true.

"Ten thousand ain't enough," Warren said. "And don't give us this hearts-and-flowers song about your patients and kids dying. You want to vampire the kid."

"Hardly that," Allan said, quickly turning back to Demi. "We're . . ."

"It ain't enough," Warren said firmly.

"Well, what would be enough?" Allan asked. He was looking and dealing entirely with Warren now. He was afraid he would slip and slide into this trap, but at the moment, he didn't care.

"Twenty thousand," Warren said. However, before Allan could respond, out of fear he had undersold Taylor's blood, he corrected himself and said, "No, twenty-five thousand. I know you research guys got your hands on lots of donations from very wealthy people, so don't give us any stories about working on a budget. Hell, we should probably ask for fifty thousand," he threatened.

"I understand," Allan said. Now it was his turn to posture. "I have authorization to offer only so much. To raise the offer, I have to return to my superiors and convince them of the importance and value of the risk. You don't know how hard it is to deal with bureaucrats," he added, smiling, "even with something like this. There are many, many doctors and scientists out there with their own theories and experiments, all competing for the same dollars. It could take me a while, maybe quite a while before I get permission to offer much more," he added. "And there's always the possibility they'll deny it, and we'd be back to day one."

Warren looked sufficiently snowed. He twisted his lips and looked from Demi to Allan.

"Well, what's your best immediate offer?" he asked.

"I can do fifteen thousand immediately," Allan said. He saw disappointment flood into Warren's face. "Perhaps, if I throw in something of my own, I can raise it to twenty."

Warren bought it. His aggressiveness weakened, but he didn't like giving in too quickly.

"You come back to us after this, you'd better have fifty thousand in your pocket," Warren warned.

"Oh, if I come back, it will be justified. I assure you," Allan said.

Warren smiled. That was practically a guarantee of a significant raise.

"Well, we want to do something to help beat the shit out of cancer, right, Demi?"

"Who else knows about this, Doctor Parker?" she asked, ignoring Warren.

"On my end, only Doctor Weber. Of course your sister and brother-in-law know something significant occurred, but we didn't know enough to tell them anything. However," he said, pausing and looking at Warren indignantly, "Mr. Moore just told us he spoke about this to another doctor."

Demi spun on Warren.

"Who?"

"Oh, nobody important . . . that quack out in Indio, Edwards, the one who writes up the workman's comp stuff. It went in one ear and out the other, and he doesn't know me anyway. I went with a friend who was getting his workman's comp jacked up. I never mentioned Taylor," he added, lying. "The guy was bored and he didn't believe me or know very much anyway so I dropped it," he added.

Demi shook her head.

"It all makes me very nervous." She looked up at Allan quickly. "What does this other cancer patient know, the one you just gave Taylor's white cells?"

"Actually, nothing," Allan said.

"Nothing? I don't understand. He's improved. How can he know nothing?"

"He doesn't know what he was given. He wasn't conscious when I gave it to him," Allan confessed.

Demi's eyebrows moved toward each other. Allan knew she was quite a bit brighter than her boyfriend.

"What about his family, his regular doctor?"

"My friend Joe Weber is his doctor, too, but the family knows nothing about Taylor, about the procedure."

"You did it this without any of them being told? Is that . . . legal?"

"Many patients in terminal states are given experimental therapies not yet approved," he replied without actually answering her question. "There was nothing else possible to do for the patient."

"I don't know," Demi muttered. "I don't know. We need to think about it all now, Doctor Parker."

"What's there to think about?" Warren asked, disappointed.

She just looked at him.

He's driving her away with his greed, Allan thought, making her even more frightened.

"Oh, I understand, Mrs. Petersen. You give it some thought. I assure you I'll do what I did before and keep it all quite simple and discreet."

She stared at him. The expression on her face did make him feel like a vampire.

"I'm only trying to do something wonderful for children like your niece," he said, reverting back to that in hopes of appealing to her sense of empathy. "You can't imagine what it's like to have patient after patient like your niece and watch them die."

Suddenly Taylor came to the living room doorway. He stood there with his hands in his pockets. Everyone turned to look at him, but no one spoke.

"What's going on?" he asked.

"Tell him, Doc," Warren said. "Let's find out right now if he's afraid or not."

"Afraid of what?" Taylor demanded instantly.

Allan saw Warren's lips crease into a knowing smile. He would play on the boy rather than his mother, and he appeared to know that Taylor did not like being thought cowardly.

"Go on, Doc. Tell him."

"Warren," Demi said.

"What? All of a sudden the genius is supposed to be kept in the dark? He knew more about all this than either of us. The kid would rather spend time with his computer than a girl," he told Allan. "Hey," he added as a new thought crossed his brow, "do you think that this has made him . . . turned him gay?"

"Warren!" Demi cried.

"I'm just asking, for chrissakes."

"What is it, Mom? Is it something to do with Jodi?"

Demi sighed and looked at Allan. She nodded softly to give him permission.

"No, no. She's fine. However, I believe there is something significant about your blood after all, Taylor," Allan said.

"I always felt it was pretty significant for me to have blood," Taylor quipped.

"Don't be a wise guy," Warren snapped.

"That's okay," Allan said, smiling at Taylor.

"How do you know all this so quickly?" Taylor asked. "I thought research takes lots of time and then things have to be approved."

"I made an executive decision and used your white blood cells on a second cancer patient."

"What happened?"

"He's . . . improved."

Taylor looked neither frightened nor proud. He looked more thoughtful than anything.

"There's something going on in your system, some unique combination of DNA that's creating this therapy," Allan offered.

Taylor shrugged. "Maybe it's the Crest," he said.

"Huh?" Warren said. "What Crest? What the hell are you talking about?"

"It's a joke," Allan told him. "An old commercial about toothpaste." He smiled. "Where did you hear that? I haven't heard it in some time."

"On a show I watch on the Internet," Taylor said. "These characters were using it to explain everything good that happened. So what do you want, another sample? I'd better keep a tube handy in case I ever cut myself."

"I told you not to be a wiseass," Warren said. "Doctor Parker is an important researcher or something."

Taylor smiled knowingly. "What happened? You asked for more money and he agreed? Because I know you couldn't care much less about helping people with cancer."

Warren turned bright crimson.

"Let's talk about this ourselves," Demi quickly interjected. She stood up this time. "Doctor Parker."

He rose.

"Of course. When should I call you?"

"I still have your number. We'll call you," she said sharply. It discouraged him. He thought he had developed a good rapport with her.

He nodded and started out. He couldn't help his sense of heavy disappointment. How did he fail to make her realize how incredibly significant all this was? Maybe Joe had been right after all. He should have said the blood was accidentally corrupted.

On the other hand, Warren looked like he might leap up and choke her for risking losing the money. Then he calmed and nodded at him, confident he would get his way. The money was too great.

As Allan passed Taylor, he put his hand on his shoulder.

"I don't mean to frighten you," he said.

"I'm not frightened," Taylor replied, glancing at Warren. "It's no big deal to give blood."

"This is a bigger deal, Taylor. Possibly you've been given a great gift," Allan said.

"Who gave it to me?" Taylor came back quickly.

"Very possibly your father," he replied.

In his heart he knew it was like playing dirty pool by telling the boy that, but the stakes were too high.

There wasn't anything he wouldn't do now to get the boy's white cells. And the most frightening thing of all was that the realization *didn't* frighten him at all.

"You realize you might have just chased twenty grand out that door?" Warren shouted, pointing to the door the moment Allan closed it behind him.

Demi ignored Warren and headed for the kitchen. Taylor looked at the door and then turned to Warren, who hurried after Demi.

"You not thinking of telling him 'no,' are you, Demi? We're talking twenty thousand for just an ordinary pint of blood. I've done it a hundred times and for twenty-five, thirty dollars the most."

"They paid you for your blood?" Taylor teased. Warren glared at him. "Maybe they were desperate."

Demi opened the refrigerator to take out the casserole she had prepared earlier. "I don't know if you're thinking this through clearly and thoroughly, Warren."

"Huh? What the fuck does that mean? I thought I did a pretty good job of getting him to up his offer."

She turned on him.

"I'm not talking about that part. Yes, you beat him up well. But you didn't believe that stuff about the patient 'seems to be improving,' did you? Whoever got Taylor's blood must have gone into a remission as quickly as Jodi."

"Remission?"

"Cure, Warren. This patient must be cured. Otherwise, why would he offer such an amount of money for what people get paid about thirty dollars for?"

Warren stared at her a moment and then looked toward the front door.

"I knew I should have held my ground," he said, completely missing her point. "We should have agreed to nothing less than twenty-five thousand."

"That's not what I'm talking about!" Demi cried, her face reddening with frustration.

"Well, what the hell are you talking about?"

"A man comes in here and offers twenty thousand dollars for a pint of Taylor's blood because there's something about his white blood cells that seriously affects cancer cells. What do you think would happen if that information got out there?" she asked, gesturing at the door.

"What could happen?" he asked, lifting his shoulders.

Demi stood there holding the casserole. It was clear to her that Warren really did not grasp the situation or else didn't care to understand it.

"Someone desperate could come after him," she said softly and nodded toward Taylor. "Or people might call and beg for some of his blood. Do you have any idea what that could mean, could do to us? This is a small community. News travels very quickly, especially news like this. It would be national news!"

"That's what you're worried about?" Warren waved the idea off. "You heard him. He's not going to let it out. He's not stupid. He wants it all for himself and his work. Don't exaggerate."

"I don't care what he said. I don't like it," she said and turned to put the casserole in the oven.

"You don't like an easy twenty thousand dollars? You know how hard I work for twenty thousand? The aches, the blisters, the bullshit . . ."

"I don't want to talk about it, Warren. I'm very frightened. Leave it be for now."

Before he could respond, Taylor stepped closer.

"You don't have to argue about it anyway," Taylor said. Warren turned to Taylor.

"Why not, genius?"

"I'm not doing it no matter how much he offers us. Forget about it. I can't."

Warren glared at him. "And why's that?"

"I already promised it to the Red Cross," Taylor lied. He looked serious enough to convince Warren.

"Huh?"

Taylor shrugged. "I signed a pledge at school. You can't give any more blood for a while."

Warren studied his face and then turned to Demi. "You're both fuckin' nuts," Warren said and stormed out. He slammed the front door and then came back in instantly. "You parked right behind me again, Demi."

"The keys are in the car, Warren," she called back.

He left, slamming the door even harder.

"What's the casserole?" Taylor asked as if nothing in the world had occurred during the last half hour.

She smiled at him. "Your favorite: lamb."

"Great," he said. "Stop worrying. Maybe he won't come back," he added.

This time it felt really good to laugh. She laughed so hard that she almost cried.

Taylor went back up to his room, and she went to hers to shower and change for dinner. Warren didn't come back for dinner. She waited as long as she could and then she served herself and Taylor. She knew Warren was in a bad sulk and was just trying to punish or frighten her, but his behavior caused her to seriously consider the option of ending their relationship. Regardless of what she considered the positive aspects, his clear disregard for

Taylor's welfare opened her eyes wider. She even began to toy with the idea of leaving the area, maybe take up her cousin Steve's offer to help her get her real estate license and work for his firm in Las Vegas. It was booming with new homes and one of the fastest growing populations in the country.

"I don't mind helping people," Taylor said when they began to eat. "I just don't like the idea of Warren making money off it, Mom. I don't like the idea of selling my blood period."

"I know. I wasn't comfortable with us taking the thousand."

"I'm not stupid though. I know lots of people make lots of money from health care, especially drug companies. Maybe this doctor even."

"I'll tell him no. I'll tell him not to come here anymore, Taylor."

He continued to eat.

"But I don't like not helping people, maybe lots of kids my age or younger."

"I know, honey. Maybe we'll think of some other way. Let's not think about it anymore tonight."

"What will you do about Warren?"

"We'll see," she said. The truth was she didn't have an immediate solution and was hoping it would just come. "He won't like what I decide. He might leave us."

"Gee, how will we breathe?" Taylor asked.

Once again, he gave her the chance to laugh and relax.

"You're a remarkable boy, Taylor, miracle blood or not."

Warren didn't return until after midnight. Fortunately, he was too drunk to start arguing with her. In fact, he barely made it into the house, dropping himself on the sofa in the living room. Taylor discovered him first and told her when she came into the kitchen.

She didn't make any effort to wake him. He didn't wake up while they had breakfast, nor did he wake up before they set out for work and school. She had to move his car out of the way.

"This isn't going to go on much longer, honey," she promised Taylor as they drove off.

"I guess there really are all forms of cancer," he said.

She looked at him. He really and truly was a very bright kid, she thought.

He shrugged.

"I'd gladly donate blood to kill this one."

"I know," she said.

She drove on, wondering how Dr. Parker was going to react to her refusal to sell any more of Taylor's blood for now.

Who knows, she thought, maybe Jodi will need it again. Family has to come first.

Yes, that would be her reason. It was weak, she knew, but for now, it would have to suffice. Perhaps she would add that after some time's gone by, she'll reconsider. She'll make it clear that what she's saying is the best he can expect and, hopefully, that will be that.

Frankie glared angrily at the wall. The second chemotherapy treatment really made him sick. He seriously considered ending it and maybe going off somewhere alone to put a bullet in his head. What the hell was five years or less going to be like if he would shrivel and weaken during those years to the point where no one feared him? He was being tortured to death with this chemo treatment anyway.

Every time that Paul Wellman went by his door, he fumed. Seeing someone with the same diagnosis so healthy and happy was truly like salt rubbed into a wound. Finally, Paul Wellman, who clearly had learned Frankie was as sick as he had been, stopped in.

"Hi there," he said.

Frankie looked up at him. The man's face was bright, healthy looking. He had dazzling blue eyes. But the more Frankie looked at him, the angrier he felt.

"Yeah," Frankie said. "I wish I was high."

Wellman laughed.

"I know what you're going through," he said. "I've been where you are. You gotta have hope."

His first thought was: I wish I had the strength to belt him in the mouth. But then, like everyone else around here, he was curious.

"How long you been here?"

"Weeks," he replied. "I was in stage four."

"Stage four? So you were a lot worse than me?"

"That's right," he replied, smiling from ear to ear. He drew closer to whisper. "They told me I had less than two percent chance for a five-year survival."

"So what that second doctor gave you, that changed all that?" he asked him.

"Second doctor?"

"Yeah. The one who gave you some shot or something the other night?"

Wellman shook his head. "I don't know what you're talking about. I went through a full series of chemotherapy, just like you're going through. Nothing else."

"That's bullshit. I don't get it. What's the big secret? Was it expensive?"

"There's no secret. There's nothing else to tell."

"You were here weeks and weeks, and then you just got better one night?"

"I'm not asking any questions," Wellman said, waving his palms at Frankie and backing up. "I don't want anyone telling me I'm dreaming. In fact, I'm checking out this afternoon and just wanted to wish you good luck and . . ."

"That's bullshit," Frankie said more vehemently. "I saw the guy give you the shot. And it wasn't your regular doctor who's my regular doctor, too. He must be some hotshot specialist they called in to help. Who was it?"

Wellman looked honestly confused. He shook his head.

"I don't know what to tell you. No one's mentioned anything like that to me or my wife. To tell you the truth, I've been so out of it, I guess I wouldn't remember even if I had been told. But I assure you, my wife would know, and I'd know today. Just keep your chin up," he said nodding. He continued to back away as if he had concluded being too close to Frankie might restore his cancer.

126

Frankie glared at him so viciously that Wellman spun around quickly and fled.

"Bullshit!" Frankie shouted after him. "You selfish bastard!"

He fell back against his pillow. The outburst and effort had exhausted him. He mumbled curses and eventually fell asleep.

That evening Nurse Dakota came back on duty and brought him something to help fight the nausea. He had just told Marilyn, who obviously couldn't stand being in the room anyway, to leave. She made him nervous. She was probably planning to leave him for good anyway, maybe to return to Vegas. Rats deserting a sinking ship, he thought. He was in a bad funk when the nurse entered.

"So what's everyone saying about that Wellman guy, a miracle?" he asked her disdainfully after he swallowed the medication.

"I wouldn't deny that," she replied and started out. She paused. "I supposed you have to have some faith. You have the best doctor. Doctor Weber's had two remarkable recoveries this week."

"What do you mean? Who else got cured?"

"A little girl he was treating. She had leukemia."

"So?"

"She made a complete turnaround. She's actually back in school already. So keep hopeful, Mr. Vico."

She continued out.

"Hey," he called.

"Yes, Mr. Vico?"

"You ever find out who the other doctor was, the one I saw treating Wellman?"

"There's no record of any other doctor or treatment, Mr. Vico. You're just a little confused. It's not unusual," she said, smiling, and left.

"That's a bag of bullshit!" he cried. Tears came to his eyes. "You're all just . . . liars."

He lay there fuming and then thought that maybe there was a miracle, but one someone made happen. They weren't going to make it happen for him, he decided. That's why they wouldn't tell him anything. They didn't think he was worth it. Dr. Reuben probably told Dr. Weber who he was and made him sound like John Gotti—not worth saving.

"We'll see about that," he said and reached for the phone.

"Where's Tony?" he asked as soon as the bartender answered.

"Just walked in with Marilyn."

"Just walked in? Where the hell were they?"

"I think she did some shopping. I don't know."

"Yeah, well, tell him to turn around and come back here."

"Back to the hospital?"

"Where the hell do you think I am, the Four Seasons? Tell him to bring me the suit I have in the office."

"Okay."

He sat up as soon as he hung up. He was dizzy and weak, but he was determined.

If I'm going to die, he thought, I'll die in a real fight, not in some hospital room seeping into the bed.

A little over an hour later, Tony arrived with his things and helped him get dressed.

"I'll be stronger once this shit wears off," he told him, embarrassed by how he had to depend on him to help him tie his fucking shoelaces.

Nurse Dakota came rushing in when she was told what he was doing.

"Where do you think you're going, Mr. Vico?"

"Home," he said. "I don't want any more of this stuff you're serving."

"You can't do that, Mr. Vico. Let me call Doctor Weber. He'll . . ."

"Don't bother calling him," Frankie said. "I'm going to pay him a visit."

He started out.

"I'm afraid you don't understand, Mr. Vico. You're in treatment with a serious illness. You just don't walk out like this," Nurse Dakota said.

He looked at her.

"Why not? I didn't walk in like this," he said. "Did I? Thanks for helping me. I'll send all my enemies up here for your tender loving care."

He continued down the hallway, pausing only to look in at Wellman's bed, which was being changed and made ready for a new patient.

The memory of Allan Parker standing there returned.

They're all lying bastards, picking and choosing who

they think should live and die. All doctors think they're gods anyway, Frankie thought.

"Let's go," Frankie told Tony. "I have people to see, and you might have some heads to crack."

CHAPTER SIX

Allan looked like he was having a heart attack when he closed his cell phone and turned to Joe and Toby Weber. She was finishing up with the children's breakfast.

"What?" Joe asked.

"She's refusing!" Allan said. "All that money I offered, and she's refusing! Not to mention the huge contribution to end some terrible human suffering, children's suffering," he added, nodding at Joe's daughters.

They both looked up sharply. His outburst frightened them.

Joe rose quickly and urged him out of the kitchen. They went into his den.

"What was her reason?" Joe asked.

"She told me she wanted to be sure her son could donate if her niece needed it again. No matter what I said about that, she held onto it. She said maybe she'd have a different answer after they were sure Jodi was doing fine."

"She's afraid. Any mother might be," Joe said. "Let it go for now. She's right. Let some time pass. It's all happening too quickly. People have to be talked into things, even things that benefit them and others. Besides," he said, smiling to attempt to change Allan's dire mood, "I'm sure you came on like gangbusters."

"No. I don't think I did. I was calm, reasonable. I offered serious money and explained and . . ."

He was fumbling, trying to understand why he was failing.

"Let it go for now, Allan. In a week or so, I'll give her a call myself, maybe ease her and her son back into my office."

"A week or so? At least a half a million Americans alone die from cancer a year. Do the math. I have many times. That's about 1374 people every day or about fifty-seven people an hour. About a dozen have died since I hung up the phone, and that's just in America!"

"Whatever results you get in the lab, you're not going to stop all that overnight, Allan."

"That's exactly what we did for that little girl and for Paul Wellman, isn't it? Overnight."

"Allan . . ."

"No, no. You ever wonder who the last child was who contracted polio before the Salk Vaccine was widely distributed? You ever think what it must have been like for the mother of that child?"

"You could drive yourself nuts with all those thoughts. C'mon. You have patients who need you now in Los Angeles. Go back to work. I promise I'll stay on this."

Allan shook his head, still stunned.

"I thought I was developing a nice rapport with that woman, but I guess I should have offered more," Allan mumbled. "I should have done what they did in the *God-father*, made an offer they couldn't refuse."

"They weren't referring to more money in that movie, Allan. Relax. Get yourself together and go back to Los Angeles."

He looked up at Joe quickly.

"I know Toby would like that."

"Stop it."

They heard the phone ring and both froze. Allan's first thought was that Demi changed her mind. They listened as Toby answered.

"Joe," she called. "It's Maggie at the office."

Weber went to his phone at the desk.

"What's up, Maggie? I'm leaving in a few minutes for the office."

He listened and looked at Allan.

"I don't believe it," he said. "Well, I heard about this guy. I guess I shouldn't be surprised. I'm on my way. Stay cool."

He cradled the phone.

"What?" Allan asked.

"Another patient of mine suffering lung cancer . . . stage two . . . he checked himself out of the hospital and is at my office demanding to see me before I start normal visiting hours. He's sort of a small-town hood. Greg Reuben, a very good GP referred him and told me about him. He's right out of central casting for Mafia movies."

Allan thought a moment.

"He was on the same floor with Paul Wellman?"

"Yeah, why?"

Allan started to shake his head.

"Were you seen when you injected Mr. Wellman with Taylor's white blood cells? Allan!"

"There was a patient who came by, kind of rough looking."

"Jesus, Allan."

"I didn't think he saw anything, and I didn't spend any time with him."

Joe sat quickly, like someone who had been punched hard in the stomach. "This guy, Frankie Vico, was in the room right next to Paul Wellman. He obviously witnessed Wellman's miraculous recovery," Joe said. "A patient who has the same diagnoses as he has, even worse in fact, gets up and walks out of the hospital."

"I don't see any problem, Joe. You simply tell him you don't know anything about any other doctor visiting your patient and tell him the best thing he can do is return to the hospital."

"You didn't meet this guy. He's not exactly a paragon of reasonableness."

"What can he do once you explain it to him? I'm sure his medical knowledge is quite limited."

"What can he do? I have a family here, Allan. A desperate man does desperate things as it is, much less a hood. You created quite a problem for us."

"*I* created?" Allan shook his head, but before he could respond any further, he caught sight of Toby standing in the doorway.

"What's happening, Joe?" she asked. "Maggie sounded very upset."

Both Allan and Joe wondered how much she had over-heard of their conversation.

"It's this difficult patient I picked up a few days ago. He checked himself out of the hospital. He just started his chemotherapy treatment."

"What did you just mean by telling Allan he created quite a problem?" When she looked at him, Allan saw fire in her eyes. "How did Allan create a problem?"

Joe turned to Allan.

"It really was my fault, Toby," Allan said quickly. "I saw this patient of Joe's and I described a treatment we were conducting in Los Angeles and I suppose he thought he wasn't getting the best treatment here as a result. Don't worry. I'll go to the office with Joe and straighten it out."

She looked at Joe. He made no effort to deny or con-firm what Allan was saying, but she knew her husband well enough to see that she wasn't getting the full story.

"I've got to get the kids to school," she said. The last look she gave Allan telegraphed her thoughts quite clearly to him: Get out.

"I'm heading back to Los Angeles right afterward," he said. "Thank you for your hospitality, Toby. The kids look great, too."

She nodded, glanced at Joe and left.

Joe sat back for a moment and took a deep breath.

"You better be one helluva talker," he told Allan. "Let's go. Follow me to the office."

"Right. I'll handle it. Don't worry. Sorry," Allan said.

However, the moment he set eyes on Frankie Vico, he knew this wasn't going to be a walk in the park.

"What are you doing to yourself, Mr. Vico?" Joe asked as soon as they entered the office lounge. Frankie was sitting there with Tony. He didn't respond. He looked closely at Allan and nodded.

"You're the guy I saw with Wellman," he told him, pointing his right forefinger, but deliberately holding his his hand to look like a pistol. "You gave him something that saved his life. What was it?"

"Come into my office, please," Joe said.

"Yeah," Frankie said, rising. "Let's go into your office."

Tony rose, too. They followed Allan and Joe into Joe's office. It wasn't very large. There was one other chair beside the chair behind Joe's desk. Frankie took it. Joe went behind his desk, and Allan leaned against the wall on his left. Tony folded his arms and took a stance at the door as if to say, "No one gets out of here."

"Why did you check yourself out of the hospital and stop your treatment, Mr. Vico?" Joe asked as soon as he sat.

Frankie glared at Allan.

"I know you guys got something else up your sleeves, something better than this chemo crap I took. I want some of this new drug and now."

"I don't know what you're referring to, Mr. Vico," Allan began. "I work at U.S.C. Medical, and I've known Doctor Weber for many years." He smiled. "We went to college together. He called me in to consult on some of his cases, but we have nothing up our sleeves. You're getting the best treatment currently available to any patient at any medical center. Doctor Weber keeps up with all the latest . . ."

"What the hell did you give Wellman that night?" Frankie demanded. "I saw him the day before. He was knocking on Death's door. I saw him in the morning, too. And I seen him just before I left the hospital. The nurse called his recuperation a miracle, and I don't believe in no miracles. Something tells me you don't either, Doctor Whoever-You-Are."

He looked at Joe.

"So what's with this secrecy? Whatever you used, why don't you want to use it on me? You demanding some big bucks? Let me hear your price."

"We have no price, Mr. Vico," Joe said.

"No price. So what is it, you discriminating or something? Playing God?"

"Hardly, Mr. Vico," Allan said, smiling. "To think—"

"Don't bullshit a bullshitter, Doc. I'm not in your league when it comes to this stuff, but I'm not stupid. I know when I'm being fucked over. The best out there have tried. Something's going on here."

Allan shook his head. "When you saw me, I was examining Mr. Wellman and—"

"I saw you give him a shot of something."

"It was part of his regular chemotherapy. Doctor Weber was unable to be there. It was very late, and I happened to be there . . ."

"Doing what?"

"Look, our work is very complicated, Mr. Vico. If I began to describe . . ."

Frankie looked at Tony. "Where have we heard this line about things being too complicated to explain, Tony?"

"Every time we faced a fucking liar," Tony said.

"Exactly."

Frankie leaned forward. "I'm in no condition at the moment to threaten anyone with what I might do myself, Doc, but I'll be back. For the time being, I have my own extra arms and legs," he added, throwing a nod toward Tony. "If I leave here today and down the road I learn you guys lied or had something you weren't sharing with me, I'll be very upset—so upset that my rage will last after I'm gone, if you get my drift. Where I come from, we value loyalty and vendetta is a birthright."

He studied Allan and glanced quickly at Joe. Frankie was an excellent poker player. He caught the look in Joe Weber's eyes and felt even more confident.

"Why not be straight up with me now and save everyone a lot of grief?" Frankie followed in a tone so reasonable that anyone would have dropped his guard.

"We are being straight up with you, Mr. Vico," Allan said. "Mr. Wellman's recuperation is remarkable, and we're studying it. As soon as we come to some conclusions, we'll submit our findings to the medical—"

"Remarkable, huh? Yeah, I'd say remarkable. What about this other patient of yours, Doc?" he asked Joe Weber. "This girl they're talking about. She was dying, too, right?"

"That's an entirely different circumstance," Allan said. "No two cancers are precisely the same, Mr. Vico. That's why we have different protocols . . . treatments for them. Men who get prostate cancer, for example, have a number of options, and the success rate for cure is different, say, from people who contract pancreatic cancer or stomach cancer or even throat cancers. It's impossible to give you a complete explanation now. Doctor Weber is doing the right things for you. Return to the hospital and let him continue."

"Continue to kill me slowly, you mean." Frankie nodded and sat back. "I get it. This is like those committees who decide who should get the transplants, right? You guys have me way down on the totem pole."

"That's really silly, Mr. Vico," Joe said.

"If it is, you're okay, Doc. If it ain't . . ."

"Are you threatening me?" Joe asked, his face turning crimson.

Frankie looked at Allan and then back at Joe before he nodded to Tony, who helped him to his feet. They started for the door. He turned and smiled.

"I'm a dead man, Doc. How can a dead man threaten anyone?" He and Tony continued out.

The heavy silence they left behind seemed to sink into Joe Weber. He shrank in his chair.

"You were right. That guy is from central casting," Allan said.

"What's that line about being careful who you pretend to be because you might *be* who you pretend to be? This is bad, Allan. From how you described Mrs. Petersen's boyfriend, the news about her son could fly through this place. Palm Springs is really a small town, regardless of its grand worldwide cachet."

"He'd only hurt the kid if he spreads it around."

"You said he was more interested in the money than

the kid," Joe reminded him. "We might have to visit with him, with both of them, and let them know about Vico so the boyfriend realizes why he should clamp his mouth shut."

Allan thought a moment.

"Okay, I'll do that before I leave."

"It's going to really spook them, Allan. You better think hard about what you're going to tell them. There's not much room for any mistake."

"I understand. Damn it," he added. "I can't believe we have to be concerned with such a thing. Especially now, when we should be entirely focused on the science."

Joe nodded.

"I don't want to say, 'I told you so,' but it's the difference between working in a purely scientific environment in a laboratory and being a practicing physician who deals with people, with emotions instead of microscope slides," Joe said, not hiding his disdain. "Once in a while, they oughta give the Nobel prize to someone in the field day in and day out and not only the hotshots."

Allan nodded, even though he wasn't in total agreement.

"I'd better get going," he said. "I'll call you right after I visit with them."

Joe stared out the window. His fear was palpable.

"We're just trying to do something wonderful here, Joe," Allan continued. "We can't let a scumbag like that get in our way."

"I understand," Joe said almost in a whisper. He turned to Allan. "But understand that's the kind of scumbag who with his dying breath would give the order to blow up my house with my family in it."

"I'm on it," Allan said.

He hurried out, as much to get away from the terror in his friend's eyes as to ensure there would be no danger for any of them, including himself.

Warren woke in the midst of a rage that had begun in a nightmare and remained with him. He was convinced now that neither Demi nor her brat appreciated him. What were those two before he arrived on the scene?

Demi was a widow with a pain in the ass kid, living a rather boring life as a beautician and a third wheel whenever she went out with her sister and her husband. She was attractive with a great figure, yes. And he really had no complaints about her lovemaking, but he could get that almost anywhere he wanted. There were plenty of single women out there just dying to crawl into bed with him.

And look at all he provided beside that. He was contributing to the financial costs of their arrangement and spending plenty on Demi and even the little bastard. Why was it that what he said went for so little around here? She was turning that brat into more than just a spoiled kid. She was weakening her own son.

How was he going to survive out there without someone like me to protect him? Warren thought.

More important, what did they give him in return? She lets the kid mouth off to him, insult him in public, ridicule him, and doesn't do much more than ask him to be nice. That apology the other night couldn't have been more phony. If this doctor wanted the kid to give only as much blood as anyone would donate, what the hell was the big deal? Look at the upside. Man, they could take some great vacation.

His rage was like a vise gripping him. He could feel the anger at the back of his neck. It made him so hot he had to go for a cold beer. Some breakfast.

After he took a gulp, he stood there in the small kitchen with its cheap imitation granite countertops, its linoleum floor, and its mediocre appliances. He still hadn't gotten around to replacing the crummy cabinets, but why do it? The whole place needed renovation. How had he trapped himself like this? What the fuck was he doing here, babysitting a widow and her brat? He felt like tearing the place apart and might have done just that if it weren't for the surprising sound of the door buzzer.

God help him if it's one of those Jehovah Witnesses or something, he vowed as he plodded toward the door, his shoulders up and his arms swinging like some resurrected cave man. He nearly ripped the door off its hinges when he pulled it open. However, the sight of Allan Parker standing there stopped him dead in his tracks. He could feel himself instantly cool down. Demi must have changed her mind, he thought gleefully. Well, okay. Now, we're talking.

"She call you? Tell you to meet her and the kid here or something?" he asked without saying hello or inviting Allan in.

"No. I didn't want to upset her at work. I thought I would talk to you first so you can realize the seriousness of the situation and do what is necessary for both Mrs. Petersen and her son's best interests," Allan told him. He didn't want to come right out and say he was here to make sure Warren didn't mouth off to anyone else about Taylor's blood.

"Huh? What's this now, a new negotiation? Because if it is, I want to tell you right off that you're not offering enough as it is."

"Please, may I come in?"

Warren saw Allan gaping at the can of beer in his hand.

"What? Yeah, sure," he said stepping back. He held up the beer can. "I don't usually drink this shit this early, but I woke up with a helluva hangover and thirst. You know what I mean, I'm sure."

"Of course," Allan said forcing a smile. He hated even being in the presence of a man like Warren. He felt like someone holding down sour milk.

"C'mon in the living room," Warren said. He led Allan and then quickly moved to get his boots off the sofa. "Sit, sit. You don't want a beer, do you?"

"No. Thank you," Allan said.

Warren fell onto the sofa and nodded at the easy chair. Allan forced as friendly an expression as he could to cover his revulsion at being alone with him. Then he sat.

"Actually, I got bad news for you, Doc. Bad for both of us, actually. She don't want the kid to give anymore blood no matter what you offer. I had it out with her over it. I think she's being stupid and he's being his usual smart-ass, selfish way. Maybe we can go at it again if you offer a lot more, but . . ."

"No, I know all that. She's already called to tell me so and firmly, too."

"Oh? So what do you want from me? You think I can convince her? Believe me, Doc. I tried." He looked around. "I'm even thinking of taking a vacation from all this, maybe a permanent vacation."

"I'm sorry if this has caused problems between you," Allan said quickly, even though it filled him with joy to hear it.

"No, no. It ain't just this." Warren looked at his can of beer and then sipped it, doctor or no doctor sitting there. "I ain't appreciated, if you know what I mean. And I'm sick of babying that brat."

"Please listen, Mr. Moore. I'm here because there's been a serious complication and I wanted to be sure you were aware of it and took the proper precautions."

"Oh yeah?" Warren leaned forward. "What complication?"

"When I treated this second patient at the hospital using Taylor's blood sample, another patient with a similarly serious condition apparently witnessed it."

"So?"

"Well, he also obviously witnessed the patient's recovery."

Warren stared coldly, sipped some beer, and nodded. "So this patient really improved, huh? Demi was right. He's cured."

"Yes, it does look like it."

Warren's smile rippled through his face. "So now it

turns out the kid's blood is more valuable than you've made it out to be, huh?"

"It's not that anymore, Mr. Moore."

Warren dropped his smile. "Well, what is it? What's this crap about precautions? What are you tying to do here?" he asked.

"Protect you all," Allan said.

Warren smiled again. "Oh, I get it. You're going to threaten us with some lawsuit or something, huh?"

"No, no, far from it," Allan said quickly. "I wish it were that simple."

"You going to scare Demi, tell her Taylor might get sick now because he was close to his cousin or connected his blood to her. Maybe she infected him? You want me to back you up with that and get her to agree for the money?"

"No, Mr. Moore. You're way off base here."

"Well, what the fuck is it? What do you want?"

"This patient to whom I'm referring doesn't know why the patient I treated improved. He knows nothing about Taylor's blood and the transfusion of white blood cells."

The cloud that had settled itself over Warren's brain began to lift slowly. He sat back to think and then nodded.

"He wants it for himself, huh?" he asked, actually sounding disappointed.

"Not exactly. He doesn't know about Taylor's white blood cells. That's my point, my reason for coming here, Mr. Moore. It would be best for all concerned if he never knows about it. I regret that you even discussed it with this doctor you call a quack. I'm hoping he really didn't understand or give it a second thought."

It came in like a curveball, first making him curious and then making him nervous.

"Wait a minute. Why are you so worried? Who the hell is this second patient? Someone important, a politician, another doctor?"

"Apparently, he's something of a local gangster," Allan said.

"Huh?" Warren smiled again. "What kind of bullshit story is that?"

"I don't know if it's, as you say, bullshit or not, Mr. Moore. I don't really know anything about him, but Doctor Weber was treating him for his illness. He made demands, threats. Both Doctor Weber and I are very concerned."

"So Taylor's blood could help him, too, huh?"

"Maybe. There are other factors to consider, but a layman won't understand, or want to understand. Especially someone this sick."

"Yeah. I get it. Threatened you, huh? Well, what's his name?"

Allan hesitated. "I came here to advise you strongly not to speak about Taylor's blood sample to anyone else. For now, it really would be better anyway. Maybe, in time . . ."

"What the fuck's his name?" Warren persisted. "If I don't know his name, I won't know who the hell to avoid."

"Vico. Frank Vico."

"Frankie's got cancer?"

"You know him?"

"Yeah, yeah. I go to his bowling joint and bar some-times. I even did some work around his house once. I hear stuff about him. He's supposedly connected. He pushes drugs for a big outfit, and he's got a goon for a bodyguard. I don't know as he's more talk than anything else, Doc. Normally these guys don't want to bring any unnecessary attention to themselves," he added in the tone of someone who knew all about the underworld.

"Well, that may very well be the truth, but as a precaution, I think—both Doctor Weber and I think," Allan corrected, "that it would be better if no one said anymore."

"You mean I, especially, should keep my mouth shut?"

"In so many words, yes," Allan said. He had sensed early on that Warren was not a man to be trusted or who cared for anything or anyone unless there was some possible way there would be something in it for himself. So he added, "If, in time, Mrs. Petersen has a change of heart, it would make it more difficult, maybe impossible, to conduct the experimentation." Allan smiled to get his point sharply clear. "We couldn't make any deals, even if I was able to raise more funds."

"Yeah, I bet," Warren said. "Well, we're not making any now. What about Demi's sister and brother-in-law?"

"Doctor Weber is speaking to them," Allan said. "They understand."

Warren nodded.

"So you screwed up a bit," he said, suddenly seeing an-other angle.

"I would rather the information we have isn't compromised and no further unpleasantness occurs, yes."

"What's it worth?" Warren asked bluntly.

"Worth? I'm telling you all this so you can protect Mrs. Petersen and her son. You still care about their welfare, right?"

"I wasn't thinking about them. I was thinking about you and maybe Doctor Weber," Warren said. "You said he threatened you two. Maybe he could do something physical, maybe not. Could be lawsuits and such, I bet. Should be worth something to you rich doctors to cut him off at the pass."

Allan recoiled. "Anyone listening would accuse you of blackmail, Mr. Moore."

Warren smiled more widely. "My father would call it incentive."

Allan shook his head, no longer hiding his disgust.

"You can call it a down payment on our future negotiation," Warren added.

Allan stood up. "I've already compromised my ethics, my own sense of morality doing what I did, Mr. Moore. I came here to give you some heads-up so you could ensure the safety and health of Mrs. Petersen and her son, maybe even yourself. That's my down payment. Now it's up to you to do the right thing."

He was shaking inside, but he held his firm, indignant demeanor. Warren seemed to wilt some. He gave Allan a wide smile.

"Hey, just trying, Doc. You can't blame a guy for trying. I got the picture. No worries," Warren said.

"That's very wise, Mr. Moore. If you need me, you can call me on this number," Allan said, handing Warren a card that had his cell phone number. "I gave it to Mrs. Petersen as well, as you know."

Warren took it and nodded.

"Will do," he said. He didn't get up to walk Allan to the door. Instead, he sat staring at the card thinking for a few minutes. Suddenly something occurred to him. He smiled, slapped his knee, and then he put his empty beer can down on the coffee table. He rose and went to wash his face in cold water.

He wanted to look at himself in the mirror to see if what he was thinking had changed his appearance.

It was that evil.

CHAPTER SEVEN

Allan was sick to his stomach. Dealing with a man like Warren Moore made him feel as if he had lost his own dignity. It was like wallowing in the mud. Had he come this far, achieved so many accolades, helped so many people, won the respect of so many of his superiors and mentors only to end up begging a man like that to protect his supposed loved ones and himself, as well as Joe and his family? How had this happened and happened so quickly? Why couldn't his pursuit of good involve him only with people of high quality, people who truly appreciated him and his efforts? Was this all part of the war, part of the test he had to suffer in order to achieve the victory he so desperately and determinedly sought?

After he left Moore, he debated going directly to the beauty salon to pull Demi aside and let her know what he had told Warren. He wanted to be sure she understood what the risks were. He would tell her that he realized his initial rationalization that he didn't want to upset her at work was really very weak. But he feared that once he revealed what had happened and that her own fears for herself and her son were dangerously close to evolving into realities, he would lose her cooperation forever.

I'm a coward, he thought. I can face germs, viruses, and dangerous bacteria but not a woman I might have inadvertently placed in jeopardy.

And yet, whom would he rather Demi Petersen heard all this from, him or Warren?

Why didn't I think of that before I went to see him? he asked himself.

He also felt terrible about driving out of Palm Springs and heading for L.A. while he left Joe and his wife trembling behind him. What had he really accomplished by coming here? He probably saved Paul Wellman's life, but the man had no knowledge of what was done to him or who had done it, not that Allan needed that gratitude. He had bigger ambitions than saving the life of one patient.

No, he had not confirmed anything scientifically. He had nothing empirical to bring back to Thornton Carver or anyone else for that matter. His anecdotal information was interesting, intriguing, but where would it go from there now? This stood to be a terribly disappointing failed mission, another failed attempt to beat back his nemesis.

The sight of the 10 Freeway just ahead of him instantly resurrected the memory of the highway patrolmen and how they had let him off with just a warning because one of them had a mother suffering from breast cancer. They had looked at him as someone special, someone who might do something meaningful for them and their loved ones.

He had come into this city pounding his steering wheel in frustration and rage and he was leaving the same way.

To come this far and get so close to the answer and then to hightail it out because some cheap crook was slinging threats was simply too much to bear. The moment he saw the U-turn opportunity ahead, he hit the brakes. He knew Joe was more comfortable with his leaving Palm Springs, leaving it all up to him, but Allan had no faith in Joe. He was too settled, too complacent. He had lost the edge. Perhaps he had never had it. Whatever the reason, all the good possibilities would just die. This whole new discovery was in terrible danger of fading away.

Demi Petersen's face flashed before him. Her look of fear, her look of hope, but also that look of trust he saw when she was in Joe's office with her son. How could he betray all that now?

I must go back, he thought. I must.

Invigorated by his decision, he sped back toward Palm Springs. He had no idea how he would approach Demi again, but at least he wasn't simply driving off, defeated. Surely there was a way to get her to understand the significance of all this. The money offer spooked her. He recalled how uncomfortable she was taking the thousand. All right. Then he would try to impress her with the humane issues, the chance to do something miraculous for mankind. Perhaps he hadn't emphasized and explained it enough, but now he would put it all out on the table, and he would do it without that idiot boyfriend hovering over him.

As he reentered the city, it occurred to him that he just might have missed a golden opportunity. This goon who had threatened them actually provided it. Joe hadn't seen it and neither had he, but it was looming ahead of him like a ripe orange to pluck. He had been too sensitive to Joe's nervous, practically hysterical reaction to realize it until now. Joe would absolutely disown him after this, but that friendship was meaningless in comparison with what would be lost. I'll use Frankie Vico as a catalyst to drive Demi to rely on me, not flee from me, he thought.

Even more energized, Allan drove on, parking close to the beauty salon. This time he would not wait to pounce on Demi the moment she emerged from the salon. It was too much like an ambush and, after all, if he was going to impress her with the urgency and danger, he wouldn't just sit around waiting for her to come out, would he?

Kiki's Beauty Salon wasn't very big. Standing outside, Allan saw four beauticians, including Demi Petersen, working four chairs and two assistants washing hair at two sinks. Kiki himself was dressed as flamboyantly as Liberace. The beauty parlor owner's hair was as styled and sprayed as any of his female customers' hair. He had a woman's soft shoulders and very narrow waist. The diamond earring he wore glittered so brightly when it caught light one would think he had a tiny bulb in his lobe. He sat on what looked like a throne near the receptionist, and, like some plantation overseer, watched his staff perform their coiffeur magic.

Demi's chair was the farthest from the front. Her elderly customer had the diminutive body of a twelve-year-old, and when Allan saw her face in the mirror, he could easily see the evidence of multiple plastic surgeries. It had truly taken on the character of a mask. Demi was completing the tinting of her roots, and even from this distance, he could see it was like working on hay.

His timing wasn't too bad. Demi took off her gloves and stood beside her customer while they both gazed into the mirror.

The moment he entered, Kiki turned, and his trimmed eyebrows lifted with interest. In fact, all the beauticians paused to look his way, Demi included. The smile on her face seemed to slide off as if it had been made of thin ice.

"Can I help you?" Kiki asked, not moving from his throne. He held his right hand up and off to the side as though he was about to give a benediction or perform an act of magic himself.

"I'm sorry to interrupt here," Allan began, "but it's a matter of some urgency."

Like some FBI agent, he opened his wallet to show his medical identification. Kiki looked at it and then smirked.

"What is this, some health department thing?"

"No, sir. I have to speak with Mrs. Petersen."

"Oh," Kiki said, dropping the corners of his mouth. "Well, as you can see, she's attending to a customer. Can't this wait?"

"No," Allan said sharply. "I wouldn't be here if it could."

He spoke loudly enough to be heard throughout the salon. Everyone stopped working.

"It's all right," the woman in Demi's chair said.

Demi put her head down and walked through the salon, past Allan and out the door.

"Thank you," Allan told her customer. He just nodded at Kiki. "Won't be long."

"I hope not," Kiki said.

Allan stepped out.

"What do you want, Doctor Parker? I thought our conversation was over."

"Me too," Allan said. "Did Warren call you?"

"Warren?" She unfolded her arms, looked back through the door, and then took a step to the right. "No. Why?"

"I went to see him. We had a serious incident, and I wanted you warned. To be honest, I had the feeling he didn't fully comprehend the urgency of the matter, the danger," he added, and her eyes widened.

"What danger? What are you talking about?"

"I'll make this quick," Allan said. "The patient I described as improving didn't just improve. He went into a complete remission. He was suffering from stage four lung cancer. His lungs are completely clear."

"So . . ." She shook her head. "Why is that dangerous?"

"I told you I treated him with Taylor's white blood cells and I had done it without first discussing it with his family or him for that matter."

"Yes, but you said that was common with experimental medicine at that stage."

"It is, but I didn't tell Doctor Weber either."

"What?"

"As I said, I was very anxious to get to a conclusion, follow a theory. As it turned out, I was not wrong, but Doctor Weber had another patient in the next room who suffers from the same cancer, and he witnessed what I had done and saw the patient's miraculous recovery."

The conclusion seemed to explode inside her and widen her eyes.

"And he wants Taylor's blood?"

"He doesn't know yet that it was Taylor's blood or anyone's blood, for that matter. He just knows something different was done."

"Okay. I'll make sure that Warren does not say anything more to anyone else. He was right about that doctor in Indio. He has little credibility with anyone but workman's compensation frauds. Now, I better get back to . . ."

"It's not that easy, Mrs. Petersen. The patient I'm referring to checked himself out of the hospital, stopped his chemotherapy, and paid Doctor Weber and me a nasty visit."

"Nasty?"

"He threatened us."

"Threatened? You mean with a lawsuit?"

"I wish," Allan said.

Demi narrowed her eyes. "Who is this patient?"

"Apparently, some local mobster," Allan said. "His name's Frank Vico."

Demi widened her eyes again.

Kiki opened the salon door and leaned out.

"Excuse me, dear, but Mrs. Cutler has to get to a charity committee meeting."

"Be right there," Demi said.

"It's impolite," Kiki added and closed the door.

"Exactly what are you saying?" Demi asked Allan.

"I think you and Taylor could be in some serious danger. I feel responsible and would like you to permit me to offer you protection."

"Protection? Bodyguards, what?"

"I'd like you both to come with me. I'll compensate you for whatever income you lose."

She stared at him for a moment, her entire face frozen. She didn't even blink.

"Will you let me do that?" he asked.

"Leave? Take my son out of his school?"

"Yes. I think you should do that."

"That's crazy. This has all gotten out of hand. Please, stay away from me and my son," she said, turned, and went back into the salon.

He stood there on the sidewalk and brought his hand to his left cheek as if she had just slapped him. Before he could move, Kiki came to the door and glared out at him, daring him just to try going in after her.

Now, he began truly to feel like Sisyphus. No matter how close he came to succeeding, that success slipped from his hands and sent him careening back to start again.

Only now he was out of ideas.

Three years ago, Warren had worked with Joel Gerda, who had a patio construction company out of Palm Desert. One of their projects was the repair and extension of the patio at the rear of Frankie Vico's home in Rancho Mirage, so Warren was familiar with the address.

When he drove out there, he sat in his car on the street, hesitant. It was almost more his dislike of Taylor than his greed that had brought him here. The kid ran Demi's life too much and therefore him. When he was Taylor's age, he couldn't even look at his father the wrong way, much less mouth off. The old man was capable of whacking him with a baseball bat and once punched him so hard in the shoulder that he had a black and blue trauma for over two weeks.

The kid was just being a horse's ass about this blood thing. If he gave a damn about anyone else, he wouldn't have hesitated. He could have made things easier for his own mother, too. It was unfair. Why hadn't anything as easy as this fallen into his lap? Warren thought. Why did a little spoiled bastard have this opportunity?

The longer he sat in his car thinking about it, the more his reluctance slipped away. He soon worked himself into a rage and practically ripped the handle off the door when he lunged at it to get out. He slammed it shut so hard that the car shuddered, and then he walked to the gate and pressed the call button. For a long moment, he had no response. Then he recognized Frankie's goon's voice.

"Yeah?"

"I'm here to see Frankie."

"Who the hell are you?"

"Name's Warren Moore. I worked on his patio a few years ago."

"No shit. Frankie ain't seeing anyone right now. He's sleeping."

"You gotta wake him up."

The silence was deafening. He waited and then he pressed the buzzer again. This time Tony came out of the house and lumbered down the sidewalk, trying to eat a piece of limp pizza as he approached.

"What the fuck do you want?" he asked through the gate.

"I got something to tell Frankie, something important, something he wants to know."

"What?"

"It's complicated. I gotta talk to him."

"Complicated? Something about the patio is complicated?"

"It's not about the patio. It's about his fight with cancer," Warren said.

Tony stopped eating.

"What about it?"

"Look. If you don't let me in to talk to him, he's going to be angry enough to have you put *under* the patio."

Tony grimaced. "Smart guy, huh?"

"It's pretty damn important, especially to Frankie," Warren said.

Tony looked back at the house as if the answer was written on the front door, and then he gobbled the remaining pizza and opened the gate. His cheeks bulged as he chewed.

"It better be like you said, important."

Warren didn't reply. He followed him up the walk to the front door. Tony hesitated, looked at him, and then opened the door.

Frankie Vico's home was a renovated house built in the late '50s. It had low ceilings compared to the homes built in the desert now. The decor was opulent, gaudy, and ostentatious, with too much glitter, cheap imitation bronze fixtures, and imitation leather furniture. Except for the tiled entryway, the rooms were thickly carpeted. The walls were a sickly green. Probably the original color, Warren thought. He could see the kitchen at the end of the hallway. A slim Mexican woman was cleaning up.

"Wait in there," Tony said, nodding at the imitation black leather settee in the living room.

"Okay."

Warren went in and sat, gazing at the eclectic mix of artifacts, vases, and inexpensive art that looked like it belong on the walls of a cheap motel. The only outstanding feature was a limestone fireplace that was obviously recently constructed. It was too big for the room, however. As Warren gazed about, he did a mental list of what he would rip out and replace. He might not be a high-rolling famous doctor, but he had talent when it came to construction.

Frankie appeared in the doorway. He was wearing a white robe, and his hair was unbrushed. He did look like he had been woken out of a deep sleep. The sight of him put the first pang of fear into Warren. What if he didn't believe him, or what if he didn't think the news was important enough? He would turn that bull on him for sure.

"Who the hell are you?" Frankie asked.

"Name's Warren Moore. I worked on your place a few years ago."

"Yeah? And?"

"I heard about your illness."

"Oh yeah?" He turned to Tony. "Good news travels fast." He looked at Warren again. "I ain't dead yet, so some people oughta watch their mouths."

"Forget that. I know you saw a patient get better pretty fast in the hospital, a patient with the same cancer."

Frankie relaxed and walked into the living room. He lowered himself slowly to the easy chair. Tony stepped closer as well.

"How'd you know that?"

"The doctor who cured the guy told me," Warren said.

"Why would he tell you?"

"I'm living with the woman whose son's blood was used."

"Blood?"

"Yeah. There's something unusual about it, maybe because his father was exposed to serious radiation before he screwed his wife and made her pregnant."

Frankie nodded and then stopped.

"Why'd he tell you about me? You here to strong-arm me or threaten me?"

"Hell no."

"So why did he mention me?"

"You paid him and the other doctor a visit."

Frankie smiled. "So?"

"He wanted me to keep my mouth shut about it all, especially from you."

Frankie looked at Tony, who nodded.

"He told you that? He said keep it especially from me?"

"How else would I know about you?"

Frankie smiled.

"What I tell you, Tony? I smelled a rat in that place. Told you they think they're gods or something."

"Son of a bitch," Tony said.

Warren relaxed and sat back. This was going as well as he had hoped it would.

"After he told me to keep it all to myself, he offered us fifty thousand for a pint of the kid's blood," he added. He had almost said seventy-five but thought quickly that too much greed was dangerous at this point.

Demi was actually trembling when she reentered the salon. She put on the brave face for the doctor, but inside she was a shambles. Thankfully, she was finished doing the main work on Mrs. Cutler. She would just brush her out and spray her so not a strand would break loose. It would look like a helmet, but that was the way women like her wanted it.

"Is everything all right, Demi?" Mrs. Cutler asked.

"Yes. It was nothing," she said quickly. "Thank you for being patient."

"I'd give you more time, but I don't like rushing on these roads. There are so many reckless drivers these days, and not only from Mexico."

Demi nodded and started to brush her hair. She glanced at the clock. It wasn't until then that she fully realized what Doctor Parker had told her. If he had gone to see Warren to warn him, why hadn't Warren called to tell her? Why didn't he think it was important enough?

Fortunately, she was running ahead. She could go to the phone without Kiki complaining. The moment she finished with Mrs. Cutler, she did just that. Warren didn't pick up. The answering machine came on, and she told him to call her immediately, but she quickly called his cell phone and again, he didn't pick up. She left a message for him there, too.

Maybe he's on his way here, she thought. Her next customer, Lila Norstrom, entered the salon. Lila was much younger than Mrs. Cutler and liked to talk. She resented it whenever Demi didn't respond or listen. Half of the work here was to behave like a therapist and listen to her clients' complaints and problems, feigning sympathy. Few cared to hear about her problems, or if they did, they used it as a launching pad for their own.

Demi put away her dark thoughts and managed a smile. What else could she do? Taylor was in school. She had to work. She had blown off Dr. Parker. Work was salvation. She wouldn't think about anything else.

At least for a while, she concluded.

While Lila was under the drier, Demi walked to the front of the salon. Kiki was on the phone laughing and no longer paid any attention to her. She paused at the door and gazed out. Another hour or so and Taylor would come by to go home with her. He had no debate practice today.

Looking to her left, she caught her breath. Dr. Parker was still there, sitting in his car and staring ahead. He looked frozen. Slowly, he brought his hands to his face and then leaned down so his arms were on the steering wheel. She wouldn't swear to it, but it sure looked like he was sobbing. It frightened her, and she actually stepped back from the window abruptly enough to capture the interest of Sharon Harmon's client, who could see her in the mirror. She made Sharon pause and then she turned.

"Are you all right, dear?" she asked.

Demi shook her head and retreated to her chair. Lila, not skipping a beat, continued her tale of woe about her fingernails. No matter what she did, she couldn't keep them from breaking.

"And you know me, Demi. I don't lift a pillowcase, much less anything that could possible damage a fingernail."

She laughed.

Demi worked out a smile. It was nearly an hour since she had called Warren, and he still hadn't returned the call. He could be in a bar, but this felt different.

Call it a woman's intuition.

Call it a mother's instinct.

Something's not right, she concluded. Something's terribly wrong.

"Would you mind if I just made a quick phone call, Lila?" she asked when she paused for a breath.

"No, dear, of course not. Go right ahead."

"Thank you," she said and practically snuck her cell phone out of her purse and went behind a hair shampoo poster to call without Kiki noticing. This time she called her sister.

"Lois," she said as soon as she answered. "Would you do me a big favor?"

"Sure, honey. What do you need?"

"I'd rather Taylor not walk to the salon from school today. He'll be getting out in . . . oh, damn . . . ten minutes. You might miss him leaving, but pick him up on the way here, okay?"

"Of course, but what's up? Is he sick?"

"No, it's not that. I'll tell you later. It's probably nothing, but . . ."

"It's all right. You don't have to explain. I've been there many times," her sister said. "I'm practically out the door. Don't worry."

"Thanks."

"I'll see you in a while."

Demi snapped her phone closed and, feeling a little relieved, turned back to Lila Norstrom, who nearly brought her to real laughter by picking up her last sentence as if it had been dangling in the air, just outside her mouth.

CHAPTER EIGHT

Taylor usually walked with Rube Martin and Jack Gibson to downtown Palm Springs, but both of his classmates had joined the afterschool intramural junior basketball team. Since the practices conflicted with the debate team, Taylor didn't go along, not that he was particularly interested in playing basketball anyway. Despite his clear indifference to sports, however, it gnawed at him that he had this attitude. Warren's teasing and not so veiled accusations of a lack of masculinity, while seemingly easy to dismiss and ignore, irked him enough for him to question himself and wonder if he was indeed deficient in that regard.

A second arena in which Warren liked to play was Taylor's relationships with, or rather lack of relationships with, anyone of the opposite sex. He didn't have girlfriends in any sense other than friends who happened to be girls, and only those who were either on the debate team or in his accelerated classes. No one girl stood out or occupied his special attention. In fact, the girls who hung out with Rube and Jack and the others either ignored him or in some way mocked him. Rather than win them over, he simply ignored them as well, which only confirmed their whispered opinions.

He was aware of it all and successfully floated above the din, enjoying his studies, his debate victories, his safe, private world. Only lately, it had begun to show some cracks and Warren's heavy shadow had begun to gain weight. He felt as if he was retreating to a smaller and smaller space, wallowing in the sanctity of his computer, his reading, his music, and private journals. In fact, he had visions of himself actually shrinking and wondered if anyone else had realized it.

It was precisely this sense of himself, this idea that he was indeed different that made it possible for him to now accept the astounding possibility that his blood carried some alien agent making it possible for it to cure incurable cancer. He hadn't fully processed the meaning of all this. He saw the fear in his mother, and some of that fear invaded his thoughts. He had a nightmare in which he saw himself in a hospital bed attached to tubes draining his blood while he was kept under sedation. He was in a real sense being mined for doses and doses of cures. When he woke up with a start, his arm actually ached.

Of course, he would never mention such a dream to his mother, who was already far too nervous about it, but it was like a nasty secret eating away at him. He wished he could tell someone and get it out. He didn't think that Dr. Parker was the one in whom to confide. Despite the kind way he spoke and treated him, Taylor thought he could see the absolute lust for his blood in the doctor's eyes. It was truly like looking at a real vampire. He had

ANDREW NEIDERMAN

done a very good job of hiding all that from the man, but boy, it was there in the back of his mind.

All of these thoughts, these conflicts, wrestled each other for dominance in his brain as he walked to town. His conscience was also troublesome, however. There were people, children Jodi's age and younger, who would die to-day, and he could have saved them, perhaps with a drop of blood, yet here he walked, seemingly impervious to it all, concerned only with his insignificant little selfish interests.

It also occurred to him that Dr. Parker might be right about how all this occurred. His father suffered a nearly fatal dose of radiation and somehow through the miracle of genetics passed on this magic. Was he in a real sense betraying his father by totally ignoring all that now? If there were spirits that looked down at the living, was his father's spirit unhappy, disappointed, even ashamed?

Taylor thought that maybe if Warren hadn't been so di-rectly involved, clearly exhibiting his own greedy interests, he would have not been so determined to refuse Dr. Parker. If that was so, was he permitting his dislike for Warren to influence him and in the end hurt someone else, some desperate child fighting to breathe?

It did look like his mother was thinking seriously now of ending the relationship with Warren. Why not give that time to occur and settle in before revisiting all this, he thought. The idea eased his conscience and put some more pep in his gait.

Taylor had a habit of walking with his head down. He was well aware of where he was at in terms of the road and sidewalk and such, but anyone watching him would think he had eyes at the top of his head. He was able to turn off the sounds and sights around him and concentrate on his own thoughts this way. He had only a vague awareness of people walking by or cars flowing in either direction, so at first he thought the voice he heard was calling to someone else. He didn't realize it was Warren until he actually hit the horn.

"Jesus, Taylor, you really are in your own world most of the time."

Taylor stared at him. Here he was thinking about Warren and just that suddenly, he appears. He had pulled close to the sidewalk and rolled down the passenger side window. He was leaning toward it and shaking his head.

"Seems like a better world than the one you're in," Taylor replied.

"Ha, ha. C'mon," Warren beckoned. "I have to talk to you about something."

Taylor stiffened. "What?"

"I'm not going to do it shouting through a damn window, Taylor. Move your ass."

"I'm walking to town to meet my mother. She's waiting for me."

"So I'll drop you off."

"I'd rather walk."

"It's important, Taylor. I wouldn't be coming around looking for you if it wasn't, would I?" Warren said, his tone not so antagonistic. Taylor took a step closer.

"Well, what's it about?"

"It's about me and your mother, mostly your mother, okay? Just get in."

He opened the door and swung it out.

Taylor looked at it. Something instinctive caused him to hesitate, but he felt silly and, more important, weak. He certainly didn't want to exhibit any fear, not to Warren. He looked down the street once and then reluctantly got into the vehicle.

"Shut the damn door, for chrissakes," Warren ordered. "You close it like a little girl."

He opened and slammed it harder.

Warren drove off.

"What?" Taylor asked immediately.

Warren turned abruptly left.

"There's someone I want you to meet first. It's important," Warren said.

And he sped up.

Lois was nearly to Palm Canyon Drive, the main street of Palm Springs, and she still had not spotted Taylor walking along the road. Before she turned to go down the one-way street to reach Kiki's Salon, she flipped her cell phone open and speed-dialed Demi.

"Lois?"

"Is he there, Demi?"

"You didn't see him walking from school?"

"He isn't there?"

"No."

"I'm almost there myself. Why did you call? Why did you want me to pick him up? What happened?"

"Just come in, Lois. I'm cleaning up," Demi said.

Lois parked as closely to the salon as she could and

hurried down the sidewalk. She was moving as quickly as she could, but somehow Demi beat her to the door and stepped out, her face flushed with concern.

"What's going on?" Lois asked.

"I can't drive. I'm shaking too much. Just take me to your car," Demi said.

"Up here," Lois pointed and led the way.

Demi was happy to see Allan Parker was gone. It was the only relief she felt at the moment. But then she was suddenly struck by the thought that perhaps Allan had intercepted Taylor. Was he capable of kidnapping her son? After all, he did confess to doing a medical procedure that was not proper. And he did look just that desperate. Perhaps he had made up the entire fable about Frankie Vico, too.

"What is it? You're frightening me," Lois said when they both were in her car.

"Just let me catch my breath," Demi replied. She took some deep breaths and nodded. "Okay, okay. That doctor from Los Angeles came to the salon a few hours ago."

"Parker?"

"Yes. He said he came to warn me that we were in danger. I thought he looked out of his mind. He really frightened me, Lois, and with Kiki whining and moaning about my leaving my customer, it was all just too much. He continued to sit out here for quite a while afterward. He looked like he was crying. The whole thing shook me up."

"Crying? I don't understand. How could you be in danger? What did he say?"

"You know who Frank Vico is?"

"No."

"He has a bowling alley and restaurant outside of town. Working in a salon, you hear all the gossip and dirt," Demi continued. "Vico's a member of some mob family. A drug pusher."

"So? How does that involve you or Taylor?"

"He has cancer, lung cancer."

"Oh? Oh . . ." Lois added as it all came to her quickly. "He wants you to get Taylor's blood for him for a transfusion. But Jodi's cancer was different . . ."

"He saw this Doctor Parker give Taylor's white blood cells to another patient, a man with lung cancer."

"And? It cured him?"

"Apparently so. Mr. Vico tried to find out what was going on, but no one knew anything, so he checked himself out of the hospital and visited your doctor and Doctor Parker. He threatened them. If they didn't give him the same miraculous treatment, he said he would hurt them."

"So he still doesn't know what it was?"

"No."

"So that's why Doctor Weber was so adamant about Ralph and me not saying anything to anyone. We haven't because we didn't know how to explain it either."

"I know, but Warren told some people, a quack doctor out in Indio. Maybe others. I'm not sure. I couldn't swear to anything he says or does these days."

"Oh, I see. He was acting rather belligerent the other night. I meant to talk to you about it, Demi."

"Forget about my relationship with him for now. When Doctor Parker returned to ask for more of Taylor's blood, Warren got him to offer twenty thousand."

"Dollars! Wow."

"I wouldn't let Taylor do it for just this reason."

"Just?"

"This situation," Demi said, impatient.

"Right, right. Sorry," Lois said, but Demi could see that her sister still hadn't grasped the significance of all this.

"Doctor Parker told me he had already visited Warren at the house and told him everything. Warren was supposed to call me and deliver the information, the warnings."

"But he never did?"

"No, and he doesn't answer at home or his cell phone. We had a big fight about it all. Actually, I am on the verge of asking him to move out. I think he knows that."

"Does Taylor know any of this? I mean about this man wanting his blood?"

"No, not yet."

"Well . . . Taylor . . ."

"Yes," Demi said, getting a stronger grip on herself, "exactly. Where is he?"

"Maybe he stayed after school for something."

"He wouldn't do that without calling me."

"He could be with a girl and be embarrassed to call his mother."

"No. Being with a girl wouldn't stop him. He's funny, keeps to himself a lot, whatever, but he's very responsible when it comes to these things. I've never had to remind him or ask him twice to do anything."

"Did you call the house?"

"Right after you phoned. No one picked up."

"Call now. We'll take a ride back toward the school. Maybe he left later than you think and he's walking right now."

Demi nodded and did so. She shook her head after the fourth ring when the answering machine picked up. Then she tried to call Warren again.

"Why isn't he answering? He wasn't working today," she muttered.

Lois drove slowly, so slowly she annoyed drivers behind her, who sounded their horns and rushed past. When they reached the school, Demi told her to drive into the parking lot.

"You going in to see if he's there?"

"I guess," Demi said. "What else can I do?"

"I'll go with you," Lois told her. "Calm down. I'm sure it will turn out to be nothing."

Demi paused.

Those were almost the exact words she recalled using when Lois first brought Jodi to the doctor.

"Now here's the deal," Warren said. "We're not talking about only ten thousand, twenty thousand, even only thirty thousand dollars. I'm talking close to sixty thousand dollars. That would be one helluva nice gift to present to your mother, wouldn't it? She's lucky to clear thirty-five thousand working in the salon for a year."

"I don't know what you're talking about, Warren. Where are we?" Taylor asked after Warren came to a stop in front of a gated house.

He saw Tony come out of Frankie's house and start toward the gate.

Warren turned. "Look, here's the deal. You just go in there with me and promise this guy you'll give him some blood. When you do, he hands over close to sixty thousand dollars in cash. We can get your mother out of that parlor of ugly women where she works, take her on a fine vacation, buy some nice things for the house, put a chunk away for you college education . . ."

"I've got my college education fund from my father's estate," Taylor said.

"Hey, costs keep going up. Your mom's worrying about it, believe me. She don't tell you everything, Taylor."

"And what will you get out of it?"

"I'm part of the family, ain't I? I'll enjoy what you enjoy. Nothing more."

Taylor smirked.

Tony opened the gate and stood with his hands on his wide hips.

"Who is this? Who lives here?"

"That's not him. That's one of his employees. He's an important businessman with lots of money. It won't mean anything to him to give us that much money, and you'll be saving his life maybe. So you can be more of a little hero. C'mon," Warren said and opened his door.

"I thought you said just promise him the blood."

"Promise and give it. He'll show us the money when you promise."

"I can't just give somebody my blood, Warren. It's got to be with a doctor and everything. You'd better take me to Mom. She should know about this first anyway."

"We're arranging all that medical stuff. There's a private duty nurse on the way with all the right stuff. He should be here any minute. I want this to be our surprise for your mother. So let's go."

"No way."

Tony raised his arms impatiently. "What's going on?" he shouted.

"We're coming, Tony. Look, Taylor, I'll be in there with you the whole time. You don't have to be scared," Warren said.

"I told you I'm not scared. I've done it before, didn't I? Are you taking me to Mom or not?"

Warren looked at Tony and then reached out quickly to seize Taylor's wrist.

"One way or another, you're going in there."

"Let go!" Taylor shouted and twisted his torso. Because of Warren's position and extended reach, Taylor was able to pull his wrist out of Warren's grip. He opened the door and dropped out to the street. Then he shot forward.

"What the fuck's going on?" Tony shouted.

"It'll be all right. Don't worry," Warren called back and started after Taylor.

Warren thought he would have no problem catching

the little bastard. Taylor was scrambling away, but he ran awkwardly. In less than ten seconds, Warren cut the distance between them. Taylor looked back, now panicked at the sight of a grown man pursuing him. His throat closed, his legs buckled. He saw Warren reach out for him, and he went to his knees to duck under Warren's grasp. Warren didn't anticipate it and tripped over him, flying forward into the street nearly face-first. He just managed to turn his shoulder in time so it would take the brunt of the fall.

Taylor spotted an elderly man pruning flowers in the front of his home on the left. He leaped forward and then charged through the man's front gate. The short, stocky, nearly baldheaded man turned with surprise and looked up. He didn't know what was happening yet, but the sight of a grown man getting up from the street and a young boy in a panic at first seemed unreal and then shocking. Taylor stood there panting.

"Please . . . help me mister," he pleaded.

"What's going on here?" the elderly man asked as Warren limped toward his gate.

"That's my son. He's misbehaving," Warren shouted, pointing at Taylor.

Taylor shook his head. "I'm not his son. Please. Call the police," he said.

"Don't listen to him. He's a bad kid, one of those clever liars. He got in trouble with his teacher and ran away from school," Warren babbled. "His mother is hysterical and sick over it. I'm trying to get him home."

"He's lying!" Taylor said.

Warren continued to move forward. The sight of him, hulking, sweaty, and angry, was quite intimidating.

"I don't need no trouble," the elderly man said.

"No trouble for you. I'll handle it," Warren said. "C'mon, Taylor. Leave this guy alone. You got to come home."

Taylor looked at the trembling elderly man and then at Warren. He realized that he had made a blunder coming through the gate. He was trapped on the property now. Warren could outrun and outmaneuver him. In as controlled a voice as he could manage, he turned back to the elderly man.

"My name is Taylor Petersen. My phone number is 555-4567. Please call and tell my mother what you saw here if you don't want to call the police. That's all."

Warren lunged forward and seized Taylor at the neck, squeezing hard enough to make his eyes tear. He turned him roughly around. Then he looked back and smiled at the elderly man.

"Forget it, buddy. The kid's bad news. We're going to send him to some reform school or something. This was the last straw," Warren said and moved Taylor forward and out of the gate.

The elderly man, his heart thumping, watched them go back up the street.

Warren now had his arm around Taylor's neck, holding him so tightly that Taylor's head was against Warren's chest. He practically lifted him off the ground and didn't respond at all to Taylor's kicking and clawing.

"That doesn't look right," the elderly man muttered.

He thought a moment and then he shook his head.

He didn't need this.

He had his own problems, and kids today were a pain in the ass. Maybe that was the only way to handle such a little troublemaker.

Besides, he already had forgotten the telephone number. He couldn't call if he wanted. That eased his conscience. He wasn't going to call the police and go through all that. No thank you.

He returned to his flowers.

At least they didn't talk back.

Not that he could hear.

Tony stepped back from the gate as Warren literally dragged Taylor through it and down the short walk to the front entrance.

"What the fuck's going on?" he asked, following him.

"Just a little family argument. Nothing serious," Warren said looking back at him. "You know how it is, Tony. Young people don't know what's good for them and what ain't. We were no different."

Tony shook his head and moved forward to open the front door.

Warren practically heaved Taylor through it. He spun around and then fell on his rear and looked up.

"Don't pull any more dumb shit on me, Taylor. I mean it," Warren said, pointing his finger at him.

Taylor looked from Warren to the large man beside him, who looked as big as a Sumo wrestler. Charging ahead and out was definitely out of the question.

"You're going to get into a lot of trouble for this," he said.

"Right," Warren said. "Get up and go down the hall-way."

He stepped toward him. Then he turned to Tony.

"Find me some rope."

"Rope? What for?"

"I'm either going to hang him or myself. Just find me some rope."

Tony smirked. "Frankie ain't gonna like this."

"Oh, he's going to like it fine. Won't he, Taylor?"

Taylor eyed the living room on the left and then turned to look at the kitchen and the hallway that led to the right. There didn't seem to be any easy escape route. He rose slowly and hovered against the wall. Warren, still panting, his shoulders hoisted, looked like some sort of wildcat. Despite his own danger, Taylor's first thought was How could my mother ever feel anything for this man? The re-alization that she once apparently had felt something for Warren depressed him.

"Now you're going to cooperate, Taylor," Warren told him, relaxing his stance somewhat. "We're going to give this rich guy what he wants and go home, understand?"

Taylor shook his head. "My mother's going to tell the police about this. You're going to go to jail."

Warren smiled. "That's right. I'm going to jail."

"Okay," Tony said, returning with some rope. "Now what?"

"Is there a guest bedroom?"

"So?"

"Let's go, Taylor," Warren said. "Show us the way, Tony."

Taylor didn't move. When Warren approached and reached for him, he ducked under his hand, surprising even himself with his agility, and ran toward the front door. Warren tackled him just as he grabbed the handle and slammed him down to the tile so hard it stunned him and knocked the breath out of him. He gasped desperately.

"Hey, he's no good dead, is he?" Tony shouted.

"He'll live," Warren said. This time he literally lifted Taylor by grabbing him around his waist and carrying him as if he were a baby.

Tony shook his head and led them to the guest bedroom. Warren dropped Taylor on the bed and then took the rope and began tying his arms behind his back and running it down around his ankles. When he was finished, he stood back.

"All right. That's done," he told Tony. "Sorry for the slight disturbance."

"What the hell's going on?" they heard Frankie shout from his bedroom.

Tony looked at Warren.

"I hope you know what the fuck you're doing," Tony said.

"It's a piece of cake. Tell him not to worry."

"It's all right, Frankie. I got it covered!" Tony shouted back.

They heard the doorbell.

Taylor, regaining his breathing, hoped the elderly

man had called the police. Warren saw the hope in his eyes.

"That the nurse you called?" he asked Tony.

"Let's go see."

They left and returned to the front door to greet a tall, slim man in a blue uniform. He had light-brown shoulder-length hair with the ends curled up like a pageboy. He held what looked like an old-fashioned doctor's satchel.

"You a nurse?" Tony asked him, mostly because of his hair.

"Yes," he replied. "I'm Gary Palmer. I'm doing private duty for Mr. Morris. He sent me over here as a favor for Mr. Vico. I'm not sure why. What exactly do you need?"

"We need you, exactly, to take some blood and inject it into Mr. Vico," Tony said. He turned to Warren. "Right?"

"Yeah."

"What? Inject blood? You don't inject blood into someone," Gary said, twisting his body as he spoke.

He's so gay that he's going to fly off the doorstep, Warren thought.

"Well, we need you to do it here," Tony said.

"Excuse me. Maybe you don't understand. Blood is transferred from one person to another in a process known as a transfusion, which is usually done in a hospital, not a home. You . . ."

"This is different," Warren said. "We have a special situation."

"What special situation?" Gary asked, tilting his head and bringing his left hand to his hip.

"You'll see."

"I'm afraid I won't see. It sounds like voodoo, and I don't do voodoo. Sorry," he said, turned, and started away.

"Hey!" Tony called to him.

He turned, again putting his left hand on his hip.

"You don't inject blood. What doctor told you to call me to do that?"

"Huh?" Tony said.

"Forget him," Warren said. "He just gave me a better idea." He stepped back and closed the door.

CHAPTER NINE

Again, Allan drove slowly out of Palm Springs. He felt numb. How he had he made such a mess of so golden an opportunity? The magic bullet had just slipped through his fingers. The monster he had conjured so many times in his mind was smiling gleefully. It had teased and then tormented him. Perhaps he was wrong to think that he had the strength, the intelligence, the power to stand up to it.

All he had left was Joe's promise to try to get Demi Petersen aboard again, but now that was almost as much a long shot as anything else he could think of doing or trying. There was no way to rationalize this. He was a colossal failure. He was going home with his tail between his legs.

For a few moments, he was wallowing so deep in self-pity he didn't hear his cell phone ringing.

"Allan Parker," he said.

"Hey, Doc, I got some good news for you," Warren Moore said.

Allan sat up straighter. "And what might that be, Mr. Moore?"

"The kid's going to give you the blood you need."

"His mother approved?"

"Everyone's approved, including me."

"But I was with Mrs. Petersen not too long ago and . . ."

"Taylor wants it this way. He's feeling guilty, and when Demi heard I was not going to ask you for any money for it, she said yes."

"And the reason you're not asking for any money?"

"I want something more important."

"Which is?"

"A little medical favor, an easy one for you," Warren said.

"What is this favor?"

"You'll find out when you're here," Warren said. "How soon can you get here?"

"Where's here?"

"I'm in Rancho Mirage. It's not far from Palm Springs."

"I know where it is."

"You do? Great. Where are you now?"

"I'm almost to the 10 Freeway."

"Okay, here's the way you come," Warren said and described the directions. "You should be here in no more than thirty minutes, Doc. Just ring the doorbell and come collect your prize."

"I don't understand. Where is this? Why aren't we simply meeting at Doctor Weber's office or the hospital?"

"Everything will be clear to you when you arrive. Don't waste any time. I can't promise all this forever. You

ANDREW NEIDERMAN

know how Demi feels. She's nervous and might change her mind again, so move your rear end."

"I don't under—"

Warren's phone clicked dead.

Allan's first thought was to call Demi to confirm this. He got the number for the salon and called, but no one answered. A machine came on with Kiki asking the caller to leave a message. He next called the Petersen residence and again was greeted with an answering machine. He thought about calling Joe but wasn't quite sure what he would say to him. He knew so little himself, and Joe would surely find some reason to talk him out of it. Finally, he decided the only thing to do was to follow Warren's directions and see exactly what the man was promising and what he wanted in return. Perhaps his luck had changed and something wonderful could come of this yet.

A little over thirty minutes later, Allan pulled up to Frankie Vico's home. He didn't know whose house it was, and for a significant moment, his instincts told him to turn around, but his curiosity and, of course, his hope that this would all somehow lead to his succeeding was much stronger. He got out and slowly walked through the gate. Before he reached it, the front door opened and Warren stood there smiling out at him.

"Glad you were prompt, Doc. Glad I caught you before you got too far away."

"What's this about, Mr. Moore?"

"What it's always been about for you, the blood. Right?"

"I don't understand. Whose home is this? What does it have to do with the Petersens? Where's Mrs. Petersen?"

186

Warren stepped back. "Enter and learn, Doc. Make your diagnosis, as you guys always say."

Allan stepped into the house, and Warren closed the door. Almost immediately, Tony appeared. Allan recognized him from Joe's office. It sent an icicle down his spine.

"Right this way, Doc," Warren said. "Someone's waiting for you. Actually, a couple of people are waiting for you."

"What's going on here?"

"Relax. Just take it all in slowly, Doc. C'mon," Warren urged.

Tony stepped toward him. Allan glanced at Tony and then followed Warren down the hallway to the guest's bedroom. He paused just inside the doorway when he saw Taylor bound on the bed and Frankie Vico sitting calmly beside the bed.

"Hello there again, Doctor Parker," Frankie said. He was in his robe and slippers.

"What is this? Why is Taylor tied up like that, Mr. Moore? Where's his mother?" Allan asked.

"He's tied up because he's what you guys might call an uncooperative patient," Frankie offered. "C'mon in, Doc. We have some things to discuss, like for instance why you guys decided Wellman would live and I would die."

"You don't understand."

"Oh, believe me," Frankie said, smiling. "I understand. That's your problem. Turns out, this kid's blood was the cure. I understand that."

"It's not that simple, Mr. Vico."

187

"Make it simple. Here's the deal. You do for me what you did for Wellman and you get what you want blood-wise to take to your research laboratory and become the winner of some terrific prize. Whatever. The kid gets quite a few bucks or whatever Mr. Moore here thinks is fair, I should say," Frankie added, smiling at Warren, "and we all go off happy. He's no worse for it. I'm quite a bit better for it. And you're on your way to fame and for-tune. Sound good?"

"This is ridiculous. It's not possible."

"Why not?" Frankie demanded, as strongly as he could in his condition.

Tony moved closer to Allan. Warren stepped out of the way as if he didn't want to be splattered with anyone else's blood.

"For one thing, we don't have the necessary equip-ment for any such procedure. We need to match blood type. Most important perhaps, this is a crime. You've kid-napped this boy."

"Oh, c'mon, Doc. Those ain't really important rea-sons. You guys have ways to solve all that medical junk. You give Warren here a list of what you need, and he'll get it. The boy's not kidnapped. He's only borrowed for a little while. Soon as you're done, he's gone. I mean, on his way home. He won't even have a nightmare about it, right, sonny boy?"

Taylor, who had been quiet, turned his head slowly to-ward Frankie.

"You'll have nightmares, not me," he said.

Frankie laughed. "He's been like that the whole time.

Shows no respect for his elders. Look, Doc," Frankie said far more seriously now, "you ain't walking out of here without you do for me what you did for Wellman. If I'm going to die, I might as well have company. Get my meaning?" He nodded at Taylor. "I imagine in your way of thinking, when the kid goes, thousands go with him, right?"

"Jesus," Allan said.

"Right, Jesus." Frankie laughed. "I'm kind of a spoil-sport about it. I was always like that. If I couldn't enjoy what the other kids in school could, I would find a way to ruin it for them."

"It's not like you're not getting what you want, too," Warren interjected. "You should be grateful. Mr. Vico called a private duty nurse who refused to help. Otherwise, I might not have even called you, Doc."

"That doesn't surprise me. He or she wouldn't have known what to do and surely didn't have what was necessary," Allan said.

"Exactly. You do, so do it. Whatever you need, you take. One, two, three, and it's all over."

Allan looked at Taylor. The boy seems as angry at me as he is at these criminals, he thought. Tony hovered over him. There was no easy way out, and Frankie Vico looked like he meant what he had threatened.

"All right," he said. He took a pen out of his jacket. "Give me something to write on."

Tony moved quickly and returned with a small notepad.

Allan began scribbling. Warren and Frankie exchanged happy glances. Taylor turned away.

"You'll have to go to a med supply store."

"There's one on Indian Avenue," Frankie said.

"Yeah, I know it. I'll be back before you can say transfusion," Warren told him. "You won't be disappointed, Doc. We promise you that."

Allan said nothing. He watched Warren leave, and then he turned back to Frankie.

"I'll need you in your own bed, relaxed, Mr. Vico. I'd like you to drink a full glass of water, too."

"What for?"

"It's part of the process," Allan said. "It might not work if there's any dehydration and considering what you've been through these past few days . . ."

"Yeah, yeah, I get it. I feel like shit and barely have the energy to walk from room to room, thanks to you medical geniuses."

He rose. Tony started to move toward him, but he held up his hand.

"I'm okay. The thought of Doctor Parker here helping me makes me feel stronger. You just keep your eyes wide open, Tony. Understand?"

"Sure, boss."

"Good. I'll be right down the hall after I get my glass of water," Frankie said.

Allan nodded. "I need to prepare the kid, too," he told him.

"Do whatever you need to do as long as you do for me what you did for Wellman. I can't stress that enough," Frankie told him and walked on out.

Allan nodded at Tony and walked farther into the bedroom.

"How did you get here, Taylor?" he asked. He sat beside him on the bed.

Taylor turned around slowly.

"I took the bus," he said. Then he narrowed his eyes. "I thought you were a doctor. I thought you helped people."

"I do."

"Yeah, right, because you're people, too, and you're helping yourself, I guess." He turned away.

Allan looked at Tony, who stood like a wall of fat and muscle in the doorway. Frankie paused with his glass of water on the way back to his room. He smiled.

"Yeah, that's it. Get the kid cooperative," he said and walked on.

Allan turned to Tony.

"We have to do some preparation here, too. I need a pan of warm water. Not very hot, just warm, some clean towels, and a bar of soap. If you have any rubbing alcohol or witch hazel, bring that as well. Oh, two soft sponges."

"Huh? You need that stuff now?"

"Well, it all takes time. Does Mr. Vico want this to take all day? I have places to go myself, and if you don't have the alcohol or witch hazel, you'll have to get a hold of Mr. Moore and tell him to add it to the list."

Tony thought for a moment. "Yeah, all right. I'll be right back with all of it."

"Good," Allan said.

Tony walked off.

Allan immediately began working on the rope. Taylor

just looked at him, but said nothing. He loosened the rope around his wrists enough to allow him to pull his hands through and then got the knot loosened around his ankles.

He indicated they shouldn't talk, and then he walked to the window and opened it as slowly and as quietly as he could. He nodded at Taylor, who moved quickly to climb through it and drop to the ground. Allan followed him, a bit more clumsily. Still without speaking, he and Taylor walked around to the front of the house and then practically ran down the walk and through the gate.

"Over here," Allan said, indicating his car.

They got in, and he started the engine. Without waiting to see if Tony had discovered them gone yet, he shifted into drive and spun around to accelerate down the street. Moments later they were on a main highway.

"You all right?" he asked Taylor.

"I am now. I thought you were going to do what they asked."

"I thought I didn't have much choice," Allan said.

"Was any of what you told them to do for real?"

"Of course not. They don't realize how stupid it all was. Your white cells were first separated in the lab, and you just don't use anyone's. You have to consider blood type. There's really no guaranteed universal blood donor type, even though some would consider your O/Rh negative blood close to it. But scientists now have a much better understanding of the complex issues related to reactions to incompatible blood types. Even donors with type O/Rh negative blood may have antibodies that could cause serious reactions. I don't know what Vico's blood type is. The transfusion could actually kill him."

"We might have just saved his life by running away then," Taylor said. "Quick. Let's go back."

Allan looked at him. He had a serious expression on his face.

And then they both laughed.

"Let's get you back with your mother. I'm sure she's been wondering where you are."

"Then what?"

"I suppose that's up to her, Taylor," Allan said.

Trembling, Demi emerged from the school with Lois. For a moment she just stood there in the parking lot looking up and down the street in front of the educational complex. She had tried calling home again, and again no one had picked up. The same happened when she called Warren.

"I don't like this, Lois. Mr. McDermott was pretty confident Taylor left the building. He runs that school like a Swiss watch these days."

"Is it too soon to go to the police and report Taylor missing?"

"I guess. They would just ask me to wait anyway, don't you think?"

"I suppose no matter what you told them, they would think not enough time's gone by, especially when it involves a teenager. You want to go home?"

"Take me back to my car, and I'll drive home."

"I'll follow you."

"You don't have to. It's getting late. You need to be home for dinner."

"I'll call Ralph and explain it all."

"I hate getting everyone excited over what might turn out to be nothing."

"Don't worry about everyone else. Besides, when I needed you, you were there. C'mon," Lois said, and they got back into her car and headed for Main Street.

Lois let Demi out at her car, and she started for home with Lois right behind her. She kept hoping she would simply find Warren in the living room with a beer and Taylor upstairs at his computer as usual. This would all be the result of simple poor communication. Funny, how she would settle for what was the status quo right now, despite how unsettling that status quo had been.

Her heart sank when her house came into view and she saw it was dark. Lois pulled up next to her in the driveway.

"Where are they?" she cried when she and Lois got out of their respective cars. "If this is nothing, someone's going to be damn sorry."

Lois said nothing. She was getting her own bad vibes at this point and didn't want to reveal it. As soon as they went into the house, Demi threw off her jacket and went right to preparing dinner.

"Maybe we should just order something delivered," Lois suggested. "You're pretty upset."

"No. If I work, maybe I can keep my mind off it all," Demi said.

Lois went into the living room to call Ralph. She didn't want her sister to hear the things she would say.

"Before you ask," she told Demi when she came into the kitchen, "there's been no reports of any accidents involving kids. Ralph keeps up with the news, as you know."

"Good. I've got some pork chops prepared. Taylor loves them with apple sauce. After I torture him, I'll let him eat."

Lois smiled and nodded, and then Demi simply started to cry.

"Oh, honey, don't," Lois said quickly embracing her. "You'll get sick over nothing and then . . ."

They both nearly stopped breathing at the sound of the door being opened.

Taylor and Allan entered, and Allan closed the door quickly behind them. The first thought that came to Demi's mind was that Allan had gone over her head and Taylor had been at the hospital giving blood.

"How dare you!" she said, moving toward them. "He's a minor. If you talked him into giving blood without my consent, I swear I'll—"

"He didn't do that, Mom," Taylor said. "He stopped *them* from doing it."

"Stopped *them*?" She looked at Allan. "Stopped who?"

"Mr. Moore apparently got him into his car and took him to Frank Vico's home."

"Oh, my God," Demi said. She glanced at Lois and then put her arm around Taylor. "What did he do to you?"

"I tried to get away once I learned what he wanted, but he caught me and dragged me back into the house. They tied me up."

"They called a private duty nurse to extract Taylor's blood and inject it into Mr. Vico. I explained to Taylor that such a procedure could have been fatal. The nurse refused, and then Mr. Moore contacted me and lured me to the address."

"Doctor Parker pretended he was going to do what they wanted, but he was pretty smart," Taylor said. "He got them chasing after some equipment and stuff, and then he untied me and we both slipped out the window."

"You better call the police, Demi," Lois said.

"Where is Warren?"

"By now he's probably back there trying to explain his way out of it, I imagine," Allan said.

"I can't believe he would do such a thing."

"He told me they were going to give close to sixty thousand dollars for my blood," Taylor said. "He'd do it."

"Demi, they could be on their way here," Lois said, reaching to touch her.

"That guy said he would kill me if he didn't get what he wanted," Taylor added. "If he has to die, he wants to take a lot of people with him."

Demi looked at Allan.

"Is that true?"

"Yes. I'm sorry," he said. "I bungled this whole thing. You wouldn't be in this situation if I had followed proper medical protocol."

"It's too late to be sorry. Now everyone is going to know about Taylor," Demi said. "There'll be others like Warren and this Vico."

"Maybe not for a while. I don't imagine Vico wants anyone else going to the well, so to speak," Allan said. "If we can keep all this quiet, of course."

"You mean if we don't have him arrested, the story won't get out?" she asked.

"I would imagine not for a while, at least. Maybe long enough for us to move to a plan B, here."

"What is plan B?"

"Come with me," Allan said. "Right now. I'll get you both set up safely and . . ."

"No," Demi said. "They'd expect we would do that. They'd find out where you are and come after us."

"Demi, just call the police," Lois pleaded. "It's all too dangerous."

Demi thought a moment. All her life she avoided reality. She was like that ostrich, especially with Warren. That's ending for me now, she thought and then turned to her sister.

"It's nowhere nearly as dangerous for Taylor as it will be once this is a big story, Lois. The world doesn't lack men or women as desperate as Vico and as greedy as Warren. I'm right, aren't I?" she asked Allan. "Well?" she demanded. "Think of us first and not your damn research."

He nearly glowed with the rush of blood to his cheeks.

"Yes, you're right," he said.

"He thought of us first, Mom," Taylor said. "He could

have done what they wanted and gotten what he wanted from me."

Demi looked at Allan and then calmed and nodded.

"Thank you," she said softly and thought a moment. "They won't come here right away," Demi said. "They would be afraid that I had called the police. Warren won't come, I'm sure. We'll get out of here. Now," she said firmly. "Taylor, go upstairs and pack some of your things. Only things you definitely need. Lois, you better go home," she ordered, taking charge.

"This is crazy, Demi. Where are you going to go?" her sister asked.

"I'm not sure. I have enough cash on hand for a while."

"Your sister's right. That's not a sensible solution, Mrs. Petersen," Allan said.

"It's not a permanent one, but at least it will give us some time to think. Go on, Taylor!" she snapped, and he hurried to his room.

"They could be waiting out there," Lois said, lowering her voice as if they could be overheard. "Just watching the house by now and waiting to see what you're going to do. They'll follow you, Demi. It will be worse for you if you go some place where no one knows you."

"She's right," Allan said. "Listen to her."

"I'm not staying here," Demi replied with enough firmness to assure him she wasn't changing her mind. "And I don't want to depend on the police or the courts. Too often men like this get away with things. We'll still be in great danger."

Allan found himself attracted to her strength and determination when she made her decision. She had been exactly like this when she turned down all the money he had offered.

"Okay. At least let me come along for a while. In fact, let's leave in my car, not yours. You and Taylor can stay low when I drive away so anyone watching would think there's no one else in the car," Allan said. "Look," he continued when she didn't respond, "I'm responsible for this. I need to be involved in protecting you both."

"Not just for the blood?"

"Not now," he said. He risked a small, tight smile. "Right now, I'm worried about my own blood, too."

She nodded.

"You should be. Okay, but we don't get talked into going to your research laboratory."

"I won't even mention it," he said, raising his hand to swear.

"Lois, go on home. It's better that you don't know any more. If either Warren or that terrible man bothers you, call the police immediately. Tell Ralph the same thing."

"I can't let you do this, Demi," Lois said.

"It's done," Demi told her and turned to get her own things together.

Lois watched her walk off and then looked at Allan.

"This really is your fault," she said. "Doctor Weber had everything under control and quiet. No one was the worse for anything."

"I agree. I'm sorry."

"Being sorry isn't enough. If anything happens to them . . ."

"It won't. I promise," he said.

He went to the front door and looked through the small window. "The street looks quiet. I don't see anyone parked nearby watching."

"She should call the police now. I don't like this."

"Mrs. Walker," Allan said, turning to her. "Your sister's a pretty smart girl. This is a page one story. Mr. Wellman, the second patient who benefitted from Taylor's white blood cells, doesn't even know about it, but he's out there with his health visibly restored. He'd speak up and be interviewed. It would easily make the national news services, and there would be a mob scene out here in a short time, parents begging for their children, husbands begging for their wives and vice versa. The lines of people who go to the Grotto at Our Lady of Lourdes in southern France would look like a garden party compared to the crowds who'd come here."

"Well, why didn't you think of that?" Lois demanded, her face straining with rage.

"I'm afraid my focus was entirely on the science and not the people involved—a consequence of working with slides and microscopes most of the time."

"Right," Lois said. "Blame it on your work." She looked back toward the kitchen and shook her head. "If my daughter lives and Taylor dies . . ."

"He won't die."

She stared at him a moment. Her anger and pain were still so strong and so sharp that he felt it cutting into his brain. He had to look away.

"I'll blame you," she warned, opened the door and went out.

"I'd blame myself," he muttered. He stood there looking after her, waiting to see if anyone would turn on lights or make any sort of move. It remained deadly quiet.

Taylor came forward with his small suitcase first.

"You're going with us?"

"Until I'm sure you're both safe," Allan told him. "We'll leave in my car. It looks clear out there. Can you kinda sneak out and get into the rear seat and then drop down so no one would know you're in the car?"

"They're going to figure out we went off with you."

"Not for a while, maybe, giving us enough time to make some distance, especially if they think we're heading for Los Angeles and my home."

"Maybe," Taylor said. He shrugged. "For now it's better than my plan."

"What's your plan?"

"Wait for the invention of teleporters," he said. "Then teleport to some place on the other side of Mars."

Allan laughed. "Yeah, my idea is slightly better for now."

Demi joined them.

"I'm going to leave the lights on," she said. "And the television set. Anyone sneaking up will think we're still here. It will give us more time."

Allan nodded.

"We'll go out the rear entrance and come around the side of the house," she said.

"Good." Allan looked out again. "Still no sign of

anyone. They're probably trying to come up with a viable idea. They don't know we're not calling the police just yet, but it's for sure they'll come."

"Wait a minute or so to give us time to get around the house and then go to your car," Demi said.

Allan nodded.

Demi and Taylor went to the rear of the house. After a few seconds more, Allan slipped out the front door and got into his car quickly. He flipped the light switch so it wouldn't go on when the rear door was opened and then he reached back and opened the door slightly. Moments later, Taylor slipped in and to the floor, putting his suitcase on the seat. Demi did the same. Allan kept himself looking forward. They closed the door, and Allan started the engine and drove out of the driveway. He made a right turn, looking into his rearview mirror.

"No sign of anyone parked back there," he announced, "and no one waiting in any cars ahead of us."

He sped up. When they reached Indian Avenue and headed north, Demi and Taylor sat in the seats.

"Where are we going?" Allan asked. "I'm almost to the freeway."

"We'll get on it and head for Vegas," Demi said. "People can get lost there easier. I have a cousin there who's big in real estate. He'll help us. It will give us some time to make better plans. You should go home afterward."

"Won't they come after him?" Taylor asked. "To get him to tell where we are?"

Allan nodded. "They probably will," he said. "I won't

be in a hurry to leave Vegas. Besides . . . Vegas seems appropriate. It's all quite a gamble anyway."

No one laughed.

It was clear that it wasn't meant to be a joke.

CHAPTER TEN

Warren looked at the empty bed with the rope beside it on the floor and then at Frankie Vico, who had returned to the seat he had when Dr. Parker had first entered. He shifted the bag of equipment from one arm to the other.

"What's going on?"

"You know what you can do with that shit now, don't you?" Frankie said.

"They're gone?"

"No. They're both under the fucking bed."

"How'd they get away?"

"Tony was looking for a bedpan or something the doctor sent him for to keep him away long enough. Smart son of a bitch, that doctor. Of course, you had me believing he'd sell his mother to white slavers just to get the kid's blood, so I thought it was okay. You're a helluva negotiator, Moore. Remind me to hire you next time I need something desperately."

"Not a bedpan," Tony piped up quickly. Frankie just glared at him. "It was a whole bunch of stuff. How was I to know it was bullshit? I ain't a doctor."

"The doctor untied him?" Warren asked, looking from Tony to Frankie as if he hadn't heard a word since he had returned to the room.

"You're getting this pretty fast for a schmuck, Moore. Next thing you'll realize is you're alive. For a while," Frankie added pointedly.

"Hey, I can't believe it. I knew how hard he wanted the kid's blood and how definitely my girlfriend was refusing. We gave him his chance, and I thought he was on board. So did you."

"Right. The kid must have changed the doctor's mind right in front of Tony," Frankie said, smirking.

Warren realized he could turn the attention from himself by attacking Tony.

"How the hell did you let them get away? I had that kid bound pretty tightly. It must have taken a while to untie him. Didn't you hear anything?"

"You heard him. He had trouble finding what the doctor wanted," Frankie offered.

"And they slipped out the window before I got back," Tony added.

A second realization struck Warren in the pit of his stomach.

"Shit. I was hoping the sight of the money would wipe out my girlfriend's anger over what I did to her precious brat and everyone would be happier for it."

"You're not getting any money now, Mr. Moore. At least, not yet. We've got to regroup here and come up with a new plan, and I mean quick."

"What new plan? They'll call the police," Warren muttered. "She'll take the kid's side against me and send the police to your house."

"Maybe. I'm not exactly worried about going to jail right now. That's not my biggest concern. My concern is will I be alive when the trial date arrives," Frankie said. "Now, in your case, you should be a little worried. Kidnapping is a federal offense. Me? I'm a poor, dying slob who was reaching for any possible hope."

"Shit," Warren said again. He set down the bag of equipment on the floor and wiped his face with his right palm. "I'd better get over there and come up with a good story."

"Not so fast," Frankie said. "If the police are over there taking a report, you'll know about it quick enough. We all will. We still have a card or two to use," he said. "Lucky I can still think. You two obviously don't," he added, glaring pointedly at Tony.

"What cards?"

"You think I'm the only one around who needs a miracle cure?"

"No. So?"

"As it turns out, my cousin Danny's sister-in-law has breast cancer. She got three kids still in school and everyone's terrified."

Warren relaxed. "And?"

"The money we're now talking about is considerably more, say a half million."

"Dollars?"

"No peanuts, you putz. Of course, dollars. We get the

kid again. Take what I need and deliver the rest to my cousin for his sister-in-law. After all that, he hands us a half million. You want to make the kid and his mother an offer they won't refuse? Try two hundred thousand. We'll split the three hundred."

The possibility of making so much money this quickly overwhelmed Warren. For a few moments, he couldn't speak. Of course, he already figured out he would offer Demi and the kid only $100,000. Then, the reality of the situation settled on him again.

"Yeah, but they might be talking to the police right now," Warren said.

"So? She's your girlfriend, ain't she? Talk her out of it. You got a lot more to offer."

"She probably won't even talk to me now. She dotes on that kid, spoiled him rotten," Warren whined.

Frankie glared at him a moment.

"Figure it out," he said. "And fast. I'm not exactly running on a full tank and neither are you. You hopped onto this sinking ship. Now you'll either sail off in the sunset with it or go down with it. You understand? It's one thing to have these doctors make promises with this chemo crap and give lousy odds, but when someone waltzes in here and promises me new life . . ."

Warren nodded. "Okay. I'll go over there and work on her, but I'd better check out the place before I go in."

"Gee, what a brilliant thought."

"You're sure about the money? Five hundred thousand?"

"I'll write you a contract. Of course, I'm sure. As soon as all this happened, I called my cousin figuring

I was going to need some muscle to fight an arrest and such. We've got a few contacts here. That's when he told me about his sister-in-law. I knew a second chance had fallen into our laps. You fuck this up, you're a goner, Moore, because we're making promises to someone with ten times the muscle I have. He is never disappointed. One way or another, he gets his satisfaction."

Warren started to nod, tried to swallow, and then wiped his forehead again. He thought he had broken out in a sweat, but his skin was drought dry.

"Get going. I don't like wasting any time anymore," Frankie said. "Minutes are now hours for me, and days are weeks."

"Right," Warren said and started away.

"You'd better come back here with some good results. Keep telling yourself your life depends on it," Frankie called. "That should help."

He heard Warren leave and then turned to Tony.

"Call Marilyn. Tell her to come home from the restaurant now. I got some things for her to do."

Tony went to the phone. Frankie returned to his room. A moment later, Tony hurried in.

"What?"

"She ain't at the restaurant, Frankie."

"Where is she?"

"Don't know. Stuart said she said good-bye like she was leaving for good."

"I imagine she took the money I had in the office. There's only one place she'd go. Call George in Vegas. I want to make a bet I can't lose."

"Right," Tony said.

"Rats deserting a ship," Frankie muttered. "I'll make sure this one drowns."

Warren sat in his car and studied the house. The lights were on, but he didn't see any movement, and there were no police cars in the driveway or nearby. He did see the television flickering on the wall in the living room, but he simply couldn't imagine either Demi or Taylor watching television as if nothing in the world had happened.

However, Demi's car was there. Maybe she was down at the police station now. Perhaps Dr. Parker had taken her. Warren didn't know what to think. His mind was a jumble of twisted images and words, everything tangled with Frankie Vico's threats looming like a storm cloud.

Calm down. Calm down, he told himself. You hafta come up with a defense.

Why couldn't he claim the kid had agreed to donate the blood when he heard about the money and then chickened out?

Simple. The doctor would testify against that. Stupid idea. Next.

Maybe he could claim the whole thing was the doctor's plan. The doctor had told him to do it, and then the doctor got cold feet. He was practically stalking Demi, wasn't he? That fag at the salon would verify it. And hadn't she called him to tell him the first time that the doctor made her very nervous?

She relied on him then, didn't she? How was she to explain that? She wasn't for this transfusion. She practically threw the guy out. He was a nutcase. So what if he was a doctor? He wanted fame and fortune just like anyone else. Now he was covering for himself.

This idea felt good. It was sufficient to get the whole thing complicated enough so that he might not be convicted of anything. He knew Demi feared anyone else finding out about the kid's blood anyway. She'd take the easy way out if it meant it all was swept under a rug, wouldn't she?

If that didn't work, maybe he would throw himself on her mercy, explain how Vico would kill him, kill all of them and that he was doing this for them, too. Yeah, that might work even better, he thought. He forced Taylor over there because Vico had already discovered everything about Taylor's blood and was coming after them. He'd kill her and her son if he didn't get what he wanted. He was just doing what he thought was best for everyone.

Didn't he always protect her? There wasn't any time to convince Taylor, so he hijacked him, but he did it to save them all. Yes, he liked this idea the most.

After he got her to believe it, he could bring up this huge amount of money and convince her that not only was this the best way to guarantee Taylor's safety, but they'd have enough to leave and start new somewhere. She'd like that. It was perfect. He congratulated himself on coming up with a solution.

Confident now, he got out of his car and started for the house. He paused when a car turned down their street. His heart began to thump in anticipation of it being a police car, but it wasn't, and it went by quickly. Relieved, Warren got out his house key and went in.

For a moment he stood in the entryway listening. The silence was heavy, ominous. What if the police were hidden here, just waiting for his return? Would someone, gun drawn, leap out at him if he went a step farther? Now he really was sweating. His imagination was running away with itself.

Take it easy, he told himself. He took a deep breath, chastised himself for being such a coward, and continued through the house.

It was quickly clear that there was no one home, but when he went into Taylor's room, he saw the drawers of his dresser were left open and his laptop computer was gone. He hurried into Demi's bedroom. It wasn't as immediately obvious to anyone that she had packed up some things and left, but he knew where her most valuable jewelry was, and that was gone.

They've run off, he thought. Why? Why didn't she just go to the police? This threw him off completely. What did it mean? He sat on her bed, thinking. She hadn't taken her own car, so she must have gone off with that Dr. Parker. Frankie wasn't going to like this, but on the other hand, he was right suspecting they might not go to the police. They probably were too afraid to go to the police, probably because it would lead to the newspapers writing a story and exposing the kid.

This was good. Vico and his crowd were still able to go after them, and if Frankie's cousin was really as connected as Frankie had claimed he was, they would have a lot of help finding Demi and Taylor. At least they wouldn't blame him. He was still helping them, wasn't he? Confident again, he called Vico to let him know what was happening.

"You sure she's gone, left the area?"

"They took stuff they wouldn't leave behind."

Vico was quiet a moment. "All right. Get your ass back over here," Frankie said. "I don't want you disappearing on me, too. We need to regroup quickly."

"Well, what will we do?"

"Just get back," Frankie said. "Wait." He was listening to someone. "Okay. We need pictures of both of them. Good pictures."

"Right," Warren said.

He went to get the pictures as soon as he hung up but then paused to think. Now that Vico had mentioned it, Warren considered running off himself. Maybe he could stay away long enough for Frankie to die. But then again, if he did run off, he'd be looking over his shoulder constantly. Frankie would have him killed just for some final satisfaction, even after his own death. How had he gotten himself into this mess so quickly? He dreamed of starting the day over and not having seized the brat, but this was no time for regrets and wishful thinking. He had to think on his feet or die. He rejected flight. Besides, there was still an opportunity to make some big money out of this.

When he returned to Vico's, he found him dressed and a stranger waiting, a man Frankie's cousin had sent. Frankie introduced him simply as Scooter. He was a tall, dark man who looked like a banker, impeccably dressed in a pin-stripe suit with expensive Italian shoes and a perfect Windsor-knotted black tie. He had thin, tight lips, a sharp jaw, and gaunt cheeks. It was only his dark-gray eyes that revealed the cold, emotionless soul inside that shell of a body. There was no doubt in Warren's mind that this guy would strangle his own mother if the job called for that. It gave him chills just to be in the man's company.

"My cousin likes being disappointed ten times less than I do," Frankie told Warren. "Scooter's one of his top men. He happened to be nearby finishing another job. I got Dr. Parker's home address in Los Angeles. We've got people waiting for us nearby. They're keeping an eye out. You bring the pictures I told you to bring?"

"Yes," Warren said. and quickly handed the pictures of Demi and Taylor to him. He just glanced at them and handed them to Scooter.

"Yeah, this is good. I'll get these out," he said and went to Frankie's home office.

"Get these out? Jesus, you guys are like the police."

"Let's just say we share resources," Frankie said. "Go get something to eat. Lourdes, my maid, fixed some faji-tas for us. We're leaving for L.A. right away."

"I thought you guys only eat pasta at times like this," Warren said. He thought it was pretty funny and wanted desperately to lighten up the moment, but neither Frankie nor Tony laughed.

A little less than an hour later, they were all in Frankie's sedan heading for Los Angeles, where Warren fully expected he'd face Demi again. He hoped this time he would satisfy everyone and live.

Frankie sat in the rear with him. He had taken a bed pillow and looked very tired but leaped to open his cell when it rang. He listened and then said, "We'll decide when we get there."

He turned to Warren.

"Still no sign of them at Doctor Parker's house. 'Course, they could have gone to a hotel or something, expecting we'd go to Parker's."

"What about where he works? The hospital?" Warren suggested.

Frankie thought. "You know that's a good possibility. He checks the kid in as a patient. Who'd suspect that?"

"What's the hospital?" Scooter asked without turning around.

"U.S.C.," Warren replied quickly.

Scooter went to his own cell phone and spoke softly, too softly for Warren to hear.

"We'll see if he checked the kid into the hospital," he said after he shut his phone.

"Jesus, you guys really are something else," Warren said. He felt like a boy trying to placate a bully, flattering him to keep him from smashing in his face.

No one responded. No one spoke. Frankie stared blankly ahead. Scooter sat straight and unmoving. Tony drove in silence. Warren gazed out the window at cars flying by in the opposite direction, their darkened interiors suddenly ominous, depressing to him. He longed for Demi's warm company, even if they were arguing.

It's like I'm in a one-car funeral procession, he thought and hoped it wasn't his own.

214

Scooter's phone rang twenty minutes later. He grunted a hello and listened. Then he simply closed the phone. After a moment he turned around.

"He didn't check the kid in as a patient. No teenage patient fitting the kid's description was checked in during the last twelve hours either."

"And he hasn't shown up at his residence," Frankie muttered. "What do you think?"

"They could be holed up anywhere, like you said," Scooter muttered. "We might just have to wait."

"No one has time to wait," Frankie emphasized. He looked at Warren. It was more a hateful glare than anything else. He looked like he might order him shot right then. "What do you suggest, big shot?"

Warren started to shake his head.

"Suggest something that makes sense and fast. Who would know anything?"

"Her sister," Warren instantly replied.

Scooter turned around to look at him. For a long moment, he simply stared. Warren felt his skin crawl.

"What?" Warren finally asked.

"Where is this sister?"

"Back in Palm Springs. Her kid was the first one who benefitted from Taylor's blood."

Scooter looked at Frankie. "Why didn't anyone say that before we left?"

Frankie looked at Warren again.

"I'm not playing with a full deck because of the damn chemo treatments. I don't know his excuse."

"Turn us around," Scooter told Tony.

"She's not going to want to tell us anything," Warren warned.

For a very long moment, no one spoke. Tony pulled off the first exit available. Then Scooter turned back to Warren.

"No. She's not going to want to tell us anything," he said. "But believe me. After I'm finished with her, she's going to beg us to listen to her tell us what we want to know."

Warren felt his throat tighten and his heart cringe in his chest. He had no doubt that this man's ancestor was the one who convinced Judas to turn on Christ.

An accident on the freeway put Allan, Demi, and Taylor on the tail end of a crawl.

"How long is this trip usually?" Allan asked.

"Four, four and a half depending on traffic," Demi said.

"Looks more like it will be about seven hours then."

She nodded. She had gotten into the front seat to give Taylor the whole back, and he was dead asleep. Despite his brave facade, the ordeal had exhausted him.

"It's going to be late when we get there anyway," she said. "Probably be better if we arrive in the morning."

Allan nodded. He didn't want to admit it, but he was quite tired himself. The tension and the driving were ticking off his reservoir of energy.

"Let's look for a motel."

"I know there's a nice one just up ahead on the left. We'll take the exit and cross over the freeway," Demi told him.

It took them almost a half hour to reach the exit. There was a line of traffic backed up on the off-ramp because of a traffic light.

"Looks like other people had the same idea."

"Accidents can really back up the traffic. I was in one that took more than seven hours to clear," Demi said. "My husband and I, that is."

"How long were you married?"

"You mean, how long before he died," she replied.

"Yes, of course."

"Fourteen years."

"Where did you two meet?"

Demi smiled and looked forward.

"I was in beauty school, and he walked in off the street for a discount haircut. I didn't tell him until afterward that he was my first."

"So you cut men's hair, too?"

"Oh, sure. I suppose I fell in love with his hair before I did the rest of him."

Allan laughed.

"You're not married or ever have been?" she asked.

"No, and no serious romances going."

"You weren't kidding when you said you were a monk."

"Guess not."

"I don't mean to get too personal, but are you . . ."

"I'm not gay, nor am I asexual. I'm . . . shall we say a bit distracted."

"I didn't think it was possible for a man to be so distracted."

Allan laughed again. Then he looked at her longer. "Maybe it isn't," he said.

She glanced at him, smiled, and then indicated where the motel was.

As he suspected, it was nearly full. Others had made a similar decision in light of the traffic jam. There was only one room left with two double beds.

"Taylor and I can sleep in one. He's a big boy, but he's still my baby," she said.

"I'm fine with it."

They booked the room and didn't wake up Taylor until they pulled up to the door.

"Where are we? I dreamed I was in a car going to Vegas," he said.

"Very funny. You hungry?" Demi asked him.

"I wouldn't mind still having three meals a day."

"How about I go get us a couple of pizzas?" Allan suggested. "I saw a place just before the motel."

"Fine. Taylor will have a surge of new energy when he smells it, I'm sure."

"Sodas?" Allan asked.

"Juices, water."

"Okay."

As soon as he settled Demi and Taylor in the motel room, he drove off, wondering what the hell was he doing.

Where are we going? How is this any sort of solution?

He debated calling the police from the restaurant and getting Demi and Taylor protection. Despite how calm she now seemed, he sensed she could easily become hysterical. It wouldn't take much. Besides, she could see it as another sort of betrayal, and whether he would admit it to himself or not, he was making an emotional investment in this woman and her son.

In fact, he was surprised at how he had put his own motives and objectives far in the background now. Not once during this whole episode and this flight did he think about how he would convince her to approve his sampling more of Taylor's unique white blood cells. Just a slight suggestion of that could easily send her off in another direction, and he was concerned about it not so much as for what it might mean to the research as for what it might mean to him personally.

It was a good feeling, which also surprised him. For a while at least, this was like lifting a weight off his shoulders. It was as if some light had broken through and he suddenly was capable of seeing himself as others had been seeing him. It restored his energy and put a new bounce in his steps. He paid for the pizzas and drinks and hurried back to the motel.

Taylor was in bed watching television. Demi came out of the bathroom, where she had washed off her makeup and loosened her hair. She wore a light pink sleeping shirt that reached the tops of her knees. He stared at her for a moment and then quickly moved to get the pizzas on the table and take out the drinks.

"How you doing, Taylor?" he asked.

"I'd rather be in Philadelphia," he replied.

Allan laughed. "Do you know who said that and where it's engraved?"

"For how much?" Taylor responded.

"I don't know. Say, twenty?"

"For twenty dollars . . . W.C. Fields and it's on his tombstone," Taylor replied.

Allan laughed and handed him twenty dollars.

"I could have told you that was lost money," Demi said, taking out the pizza and fixing Taylor a piece. She handed it to him with a juice drink and then sat at the table to eat with Allan.

Taylor remained interested in his television program.

"How long have you been with Mr. Moore?" Allan asked, speaking softly. It was as if he were walking over thin ice.

"Too long, obviously." She shrugged. "We had a lot of fun in the beginning. I was attracted to his laid-back, que sera, sera attitude after going through what Taylor and I had gone through. It's easy to blind yourself or deliberately ignore someone's flaws when you're in the state of mind I was in." She paused. "I guess I sound like someone reaching for excuses."

"Not at all. It makes sense."

"And," she said, smiling, "I'm sure you're familiar with that saying, 'It's easier for a woman over 35 to be killed by a terrorist than find a good romantic relationship.'"

Allan laughed.

"I never heard that, but don't go by me. I just found out women were given the right to vote."

Demi laughed and then looked at him as if she really was looking at him for the first time. It made him blush, which surprised him even more than it did her.

"You really never had a serious romantic relationship, Doctor Parker?"

"Please, call me Allan. I think we've been through enough to do away with anything formal. To answer your question, however, I went steady for two days in the ninth grade until she told me she hated to brush her teeth."

Demi laughed.

"Aren't you the particular one?"

"No. I guess I'm a devout coward when it comes to re-lationships, and I rationalize by telling myself it will take me away from my goals and what I hope is my destiny. That's about all the self-analysis I'm capable of doing."

"Maybe it's enough," she said.

They just looked at each other for a long moment. Then she stood.

"Want any more of this?"

"No. Thank you."

Demi cleared off the table and threw the boxes and empty cups in the garbage.

"This cleaning thing. It's instinctive," she said, seeing how Allan was watching her straighten up a motel room.

He laughed. They both looked at Taylor and saw he had fallen asleep. Gently, Demi took everything away from him and fixed his blanket.

"We'd better go to sleep, too," Allan said. He rose and went into the bathroom.

When he came out, he found Demi had turned off the television and left only his light. He left his briefs on and crawled into his bed. After he turned off his light, some car headlights swept the wall and then it became very quiet. He lay there in the darkness wondering how this was all going to end.

In the dim light filtering through the curtains, he could see Demi was still awake.

Surely, he thought, she's wondering the same thing.

CHAPTER ELEVEN

Less than an hour after he had fallen asleep, Allan felt Demi's hand on his arm and opened his eyes. She was kneeling at the side of his bed.

"What's wrong?" he asked.

"I'm sorry. I can't sleep. I think I made a terrible mistake."

She sounded on the verge of tears. He pulled himself into a sitting position against his pillows, and Demi rose to sit on the side of his bed.

"What do you mean?"

"This flight, running away. If these people are as ruthless as you say, they'll only come after us, no matter what or where we go."

He nodded. "I imagine they will."

"Why didn't you try harder to stop me, to change my mind, Allan?"

"Well, if you remember, I did suggest you come with me, but I thought if I was adamant you'd think I had only one reason to care. I'd only convince you of that by insisting and insisting."

ANDREW NEIDERMAN

"But that was true though, wasn't it? You had only one reason."

"In the beginning, it was true," he admitted. "But . . ."

"But what?"

"I began to see you as I should have seen you from the start, Demi, both of you, as people and not specimens or research objects."

She nodded.

"And then it became even more important to me that you . . ."

"What?"

"Trusted me. If it meant going along with what you wanted, well, that's what I would do. Look," he added, "I'm not good at this sort of thing, so if I sound stupid . . ."

"What sort of thing, Allan?"

He looked at her. In the vague light, she seemed to be even more attractive to him, more of a beautiful fantasy. Her nightshirt rose on her legs, revealing more of her glistening skin. Her breasts seemed to lift and become even firmer, her nipples even more than vaguely outlined.

"Expressing myself, my feelings," he replied. "Especially when it comes to my feelings for you. I'm surprised myself at how strong they are, but . . ."

"Sometimes, it's better said in other ways."

"Yes, but I'm still afraid that anything I do will be misinterpreted, will be seen as conniving or manipulative and not sincere."

"Let me be the judge of that," she replied.

He smiled, nodded, and leaned forward. She did too

224

and they kissed, softly at first, parted, but did not pull back. They kissed again. He brought his hands to her upper arms and kept her close. When he leaned back, she leaned with him, keeping her cheeks against his. He kissed her again. She moaned softly and brushed his forehead with her lips. He kissed her neck, and then she pulled back and rose. He was disappointed until he saw her lift the blanket and gently slide in beside him.

"That felt sincere enough," she whispered. "I think I trust you."

He laughed. "It was sincere."

"I'm scared, Allan," she said. "Hold me."

He embraced her, and they kissed again. She looked back at Taylor. He was on his side with his back to them.

"He went through some terrible time," Allan said. "I gotta say you have one helluva brave kid there."

"I know. He's my rock. What should we do?"

"We pretty much have no choice now, Demi. We have to go to the police. I know you're terrified of what will happen when the story gets out, but I can arrange for Taylor to be insulated."

"By doing what, being a research guinea pig?"

"Not exactly, no, but I do need to attract the interest of those who have it within their power to help us."

"I wouldn't want him locked up for his own protection. It's important he has a normal life."

"It's not too normal at the moment, Demi."

"I know, but how would it ever be if we do what you're suggesting?"

"It would be kind of like the federal witness protection program, I imagine."

"You mean, new identities, lives? How can a hospital research group arrange such a thing?"

"One of the foundations that supports our work has some influential people running it. I'm confident I can get you and Taylor the protection you need."

Demi lowered herself against him again.

"What would I do?"

"Whatever you want, what you're doing now, if you want."

"No. I'd rather go to school, learn to do something more significant. Maybe something to do with the health industry, and I don't mean a secretary in an HMO or something."

Allan nodded. "I know I can arrange something there. Who knows? Maybe someday soon you'll be working alongside me."

They heard Taylor moan.

"I'd better get back over there. He's too old now to see his mother in bed with another man so soon after leaving the last one."

"Next time we'll get two rooms."

She started to get out, and he seized her hand. She leaned back and kissed him again.

"I mean it. I mean that there'll be a next time."

"Good," she whispered and crawled in beside Taylor, but she faced Allan.

"That wasn't exactly the right formula for helping someone get to sleep," he whispered.

She laughed softly.

"Sure it was, Allan. You just fantasize."

"With the real thing a few feet away?"

She looked back at Taylor again.

"Maybe . . ."

"No, no. I'm just teasing," he whispered. "We both could use some sleep. We should get out of here as soon as we can and go first to the police back in Palm Springs."

"Okay."

She turned on her back and looked up at the ceiling.

He did the same, and although they both closed their eyes, it felt as if they were still looking at each other.

"Let me try first, okay?" Warren asked Frankie when they pulled up in front of the Walkers' house. There was only a lamp on in what Warren knew to be the living room of the two-story Spanish-style home. It was set on a small rise just outside of Palm Springs in one of the older but more expensive neighborhoods. Each house had nearly an acre lot, and each had literally tens of thousands of dollars in landscaping, palm trees, and outside lighting.

Every other room in the house was in darkness. It was just after midnight.

"Go in first? What are you worried about, losing their friendship? I told you I have no time to waste," Frankie replied. "You can ask the questions, but Scooter will be right beside you to make sure we get the answers we need and need now."

"This guy is connected to some big shots here," Warren warned. Frankie just stared at him deadpan a moment.

227

"Scooter?" Frankie said.

"I'm trembling in my shoes."

Tony laughed. Scooter opened his door. Tony opened the door for Frankie and helped him out.

I'm in a free fall, Warren thought, going deeper and deeper until there's no way back.

"Lead the way, big shot," Frankie ordered.

Warren got out and started toward the Walkers' front door. The blinking lights of a commercial jet beginning its descent for Los Angeles were nearly lost among the stars in the eastern sky. Warren suddenly longed to be sitting on the plane, far above the mess he had made for himself. He pushed the door buzzer and looked at Scooter in the shadows just off to his left. The man seemed to have no face.

Tony and Frankie remained a few feet behind.

"Push it again," Frankie ordered.

Warren did so, and a light went on above them in what he knew to be the Walkers' master bedroom. That was followed by another light above the stairway and then another in the entryway. Moments later, Ralph Walker, in his robe and slippers, opened the door. It was apparent from the expression on his face the moment he saw Warren that his wife had revealed the events occurring over the past half-dozen hours. His rage was such that his eyes didn't drift from Warren's face, and he didn't see Scooter standing just off what was his right, nor did he seem to notice Tony and Frankie a few feet behind.

"What do you want, Warren? Lois told me what you . . ."

He recoiled when Scooter moved into the light above the door.

"Who's this?"

He looked past them now and saw Frankie Vico. He knew who he was.

"What the hell is this?" he demanded, trying to sound as unafraid and as indignant as he could. "You know the time?"

"Believe me, I know the time," Frankie said.

"Look, we need to know where Demi's gone, Ralph. This whole thing is just a terrible misunderstanding. I have to get things straightened out immediately. I need to know where she is now," Warren said quickly and then tried to smile and added, "She'll be happy with what is being proposed now, very happy."

Ralph heard everything Warren said, but he seemed mesmerized by Scooter's appearance. He didn't move, didn't blink. Then he swallowed hard enough for his Adam's apple to bounce and shook his head.

"You all need to get off my property before I call the police," he said. "I'm upset that Demi hasn't done so yet, but if I have my way, she will, so I'd think about the trouble you're already in and not add to it, if I were you."

"Now why would you want to a thing like that, Mr. Walker?" Scooter asked, nudging Warren out of the way and stepping into the doorway.

Ralph retreated. He eyed Scooter's hands. The fingers were long and thin with a glittering diamond ring in a gold setting on the pinky of his right hand. He undid his suit jacket. The handle of a pistol in a shoulder holster was just visible.

"Who is this, Warren?" Ralph asked as if ignoring Scooter would eradicate his existence.

"This is something that's easy or something that's hard," Scooter said. "When I say easy and hard, I mean easy or hard for you, your wife, and your daughter."

Ralph looked like he lost the ability to speak. His lips moved, but no sound emerged, and his eyes widened with abject terror.

"It's not just me who's asking you, Ralph," Warren offered, trying to sound apologetic.

"He's right about that," Frankie shouted and moved closer with Tony.

Scooter smiled.

Close to a panic, Ralph straightened up and reached for the doorknob. "All of you get off my property now!"

He started to close the door on them, but Scooter put his left foot out and stopped it. Then, with lightning speed, so fast that even Warren was surprised and jumped, Scooter shot his long, right arm out like a sword and seized Ralph's throat. His fingers were squeezing so hard that they looked like they were sinking through Ralph's skin. Ralph gagged and reached defensively for Scooter's wrist, but Scooter grabbed his hair with his left hand and jerked Ralph forward and stepped into the house. He nodded at Warren, Tony, and Frankie, who immediately followed. Tony closed the door behind them.

Scooter continued to hold onto Ralph, squeezing

harder on his throat until Ralph went to his knees. He had his hands on Scooter's arm, but it was like a little girl trying to break the grip of a professional wrestler.

Ralph's face quickly turned an incredibly dark shade of red, and when he looked up, Warren could see his lips were rapidly fading into a dark blue. The realization that he was watching Ralph being murdered triggered him to act. It was one thing to force the brat to give up some blood, but another to participate in a truly cold-blooded killing, especially of someone who at one point was nearly a relative. He grabbed Scooter's left arm at the elbow and pulled hard. Scooter didn't release Ralph's hair, but he turned angrily to Warren.

Not the horror he had seen in a movie, or the horror he had read in a book, or even had experienced in a nightmare prepared him for the cold, brutal look in Scooter's eyes. It was like looking at the face of Death itself. He released his grip.

"Don't kill him. It will make it harder to get the information. She'll be in shock, hysterical," he hurriedly explained.

"Don't interfere, Mr. Moore," Frankie said. "Scooter knows what to do here."

"I'm not interfering. I'm just saying we'll get what we want from his wife, I'm sure."

The cooling in Scooter's eyes encouraged Warren to continue with his pleading and logic.

"It will only make this longer, Frankie. She'll faint or something, and we'll be here the rest of the damn night."

"Let Scooter decide," Frankie said.

Tony stepped up beside Warren obviously to make sure he didn't do anything more to interfere.

Scooter relaxed his grip on Ralph's throat, but tugged his hair so he would fall to the floor where he writhed and coughed.

"Ralph?" they heard from the top of the stairway. "Who's there? Ralph? What's going on?"

Scooter took out his pistol and stepped on Ralph's shoulder to drive him face forward on the floor. Lois came down the stairway quickly. She was in her robe. The moment she saw the scene in the entryway, she screamed. Scooter put his left hand up like a traffic cop and pointed his pistol at Ralph. It was enough to stop her from screaming, but she looked like she was tottering on the stairway.

"Get her down here," Scooter ordered. Warren moved before Tony and stepped over Ralph. He approached the stairway with his arms out, smiling.

"C'mon down, Lois. It's going to be all right. Just come down," he pleaded and beckoned with his hand. She glared at him, looked at Scooter, Tony, Frankie, and Ralph, and took a few timid steps toward Warren. He smiled and reached for her hand.

"Who are these people? What have you done?" she asked him, pulling her hand back from his. "What are you doing to us?"

"Just calm down, Lois. It will be better for everyone if you just calm down," Warren said. He tried to telegraph the danger with his eyes and look like he was interceding on her and Ralph's behalf, but she glared back at him with unadulterated disgust and hate.

Scooter took his foot off Ralph and beckoned for Lois to come closer. Warren reached again for Lois's hand, this time more forcefully. He then led her down the remaining steps. Ralph groaned and rose to his feet slowly, rubbing his reddened neck. He looked more embarrassed than anything but bravely moved to Lois's side and pushed Warren away.

"What do you want?" he asked.

"He's already told you," Frankie said. "We want to know where Mrs. Petersen and her son have gone, and I can assure you," Frankie continued, nodding at Scooter, "that it would be very bad for you if you didn't tell us the truth."

"We don't know where she's gone," Ralph said. "After what he did," he added, pointing at Warren, "she panicked and ran off."

"There's a critical time factor here," Scooter said. "Otherwise, we'd be happy to play tiddlywinks with you for a while." He looked at Warren. "I was going to impress . . . Lois, is it? Lois here with the urgency by choking the life out of Ralph. It is Ralph, right? Yes, Ralph. But, Mr. Moore interceded without permission and temporarily delayed my efforts to clearly illustrate how serious we are, and how impatient."

"We're telling you the truth!" Lois cried. "My sister was in a panic. She thought it was better for them to leave the area. She didn't want any more attention drawn to herself—and especially her son," she added quickly.

"And you're telling us you don't know where your sister has gone?" Scooter asked skeptically.

"I asked her where she intended to go, but she was afraid of just something like this so she said she would call me when she got there. That's the truth. Please, believe me and leave us alone."

She moved quickly to Ralph's side and took his arm.

The noise finally woke Jodi, who came out of her upstairs bedroom and to the stairway. She wiped her eyes and gazed down at the confusing scene below.

"Mommy!"

Lois rushed up the stairway to embrace her.

"Bring her down," Scooter commanded. He waved at them with his pistol. "Now."

"She told you the truth. Just leave us alone. We can't help you," Ralph pleaded. He took a step toward Scooter, who then raised his pistol.

"Ralph!" Lois screamed.

"Bring her down," Scooter said firmly.

Tottering on losing consciousness, Lois carried Jodi most of the way down and then lowered her to the last few steps.

"And your name is?" Scooter asked.

Jodi looked at her mother and then said, "Jodi."

"Jodi," Scooter said, smiling. "Nice name. Perfect. Okay, so we're all settled in now and back to why we came." He looked at his watch. "I'm about two minutes over what I had allotted for this little venture, which is truly disappointing." He stepped toward Ralph but kept his attention on Jodi and Lois and smiled.

She gasped and pulled Jodi closer to her.

"Where," Scooter said slowly, "is your sister and her son? Exactly."

"I told you the truth. I'm not sure . . . she could've gone to Las Vegas or maybe San Francisco. We have relatives in both places."

"Have you spoken with her since she left?"

"No. She specifically forbid me calling her. I told you. She said she would call me."

"And she left with that doctor?" Frankie asked.

"Yes. She left with him."

Scooter raised the pistol and pointed it at Ralph's head. "One more chance. Tell us where she is."

"I can't! I don't know! Please, please!" Lois pleaded. Scooter brought back the hammer on the pistol. "Oh, God, help us!"

He lowered the hammer and turned to Frankie. "My expert opinion in these matters convinces me she's telling the truth."

"Fuck," Frankie said. He glared more angrily at Warren than anyone else. "Some great idea."

Everyone stood silently for a moment. Ralph moved to Lois and Jodi's side. Then Frankie looked up sharply at Warren.

"How'd you get that doctor to come to my place in the first place?"

"I told you. I teased him with the possibility of getting the blood he wanted. I told him I needed a small medical favor first and . . ."

"How did you tell him?"

"How?" Warren looked at Scooter as if he hoped he would provide the answer Frankie demanded.

"I . . . called him."

"Where, schmuck?"

"On his cell phone."

"You had the guy's cell phone number all this time?" Scooter asked.

"Yeah, sure." Warren dug frantically into his pocket and came up with the card Allan Parker had given him.

Scooter snatched it and looked at it. Then he turned to Frankie and shook his head.

"This guy is a like a cement shoe on your foot."

Frankie nodded.

Scooter turned back to Lois.

"We're going to need you to convince this doctor to bring your sister and her son home," Scooter told her.

Lois started to shake her head.

Without any hesitation, Scooter lifted his pistol again, but this time pointed it at Warren and shot him in the face. Warren's head exploded, and he flew back over the coffee table, crumbling against the sofa.

Lois and Jodi screamed. Ralph's eyes bulged. He embraced his wife and daughter, and the three of them cowered back. Even Tony looked overwhelmed. Frankie simply smirked. Scooter turned to him and shook his head.

"I'm losing what little faith I had in humanity rapidly," he said.

Frankie nodded.

"Now then, Lois, where were we? Oh yes. You're going

to make a call to this doctor and convince him to bring your sister and your nephew back ASAP. You're going to warn them not to call the police because there is a really good chance that your whole family, with your daughter first, will be shot. Can you remember all that?"

Lois couldn't speak. She could barely nod.

"Great. Ralph boy. Go with Tony here and find something to throw over this body. I hate looking at my work, and all sorts of odors will soon arise and we might have to be here a while. See about some coffee, too, Tony, and whatever they have to go with it. I'm a little hungry. This work always makes me a little hungry."

Ralph held onto Lois.

"Do what he says," she whispered. "I'll be all right."

He nodded and stepped away. Before heading for the kitchen, he looked down at Warren.

"You bastard," he said. "I wish you weren't dead so I could kill you myself."

Scooter roared with laughter.

"I like your husband. C'mon, Lois," he said, patting the big cushioned chair next to the table with the phone. "Make yourself comfortable, and then make the most important call of your life and your husband's and daughter's lives."

Ralph looked back at her. He could see the turmoil in her face. She was endangering her sister to save her own family. It killed him that he could do nothing to stop it.

She lowered Jodi to the floor and then took her hand as she went to the chair.

"This turned out to be a little harder than I thought. I

expect you'll testify to my getting a bonus or something after all this, Frankie," Scooter said.

"Don't worry about it. Get it done, and I'll give it to you myself," Frankie told him.

Allan had put his cell phone on vibrate so it took a while for him to realize he was getting a call. He got out of bed quickly to answer. Demi and Taylor were asleep.

"Allan Parker," he said in a low voice with his back to Demi and Taylor.

"Doctor Parker. It's Lois Walker, Demi's sister."

"Yes?"

"You must bring them back now. Come directly to my home. Please."

"What? Why?"

"My life and my husband and daughter's lives are in great danger. How far away are you?"

"I don't understand. Why are you and your family in danger?"

"They have come here," she said. He could hear how difficult it was for her to speak. "If you call the police, we'll . . . they'll . . . please, just tell Demi how much I need her to do this. Come and do what they want. Please. How far away are you?" she repeated.

"They've come? You mean Warren's there?" Allan asked, now raging with anger. "He's threatening you and your family?"

"Yes, he's here, Doctor Parker. He brought the others here tonight."

"Put him on the phone. I'll put an end to this right away, believe me."

"I can't."

"Why not?"

"He's . . . dead. He was shot right in front of my daughter a few minutes ago," Lois said. Allan sensed someone was giving her permission or urging her to tell him how bad it was. "She's practically in shock. We all are."

"Shot? They shot him?"

Lois began to sob.

"All right. Take it easy, Mrs. Walker. Tell whomever is there with you that we'll be starting back. We're two or three hours away, and your sister and nephew are asleep."

He heard her relaying the information to someone. There was some indistinct mumbling, a discussion being carried on. He looked at Demi, who had woken up because he had raised his voice.

"Who is it, Allan?"

He didn't respond. She sat up.

"Allan?"

He held up his hand.

"They want to know where you are, what direction you took?"

"Why?"

"Please, Doctor Parker."

"We were heading for Vegas, but there was a major traffic jam so we pulled off the highway."

"Allan!" Demi cried now and got out of bed.

Taylor groaned and turned in the bed.

Lois spoke to someone again and then came back on.

"They've decided they want you to meet them somewhere rather than come here. You'll be called on your cell phone in twenty minutes. They are warning you once more not to call the police. They say they have ways to know immediately."

"Wait," Allan said. "If we do what they say, how can I be sure you and your family will be left alone?"

She relayed his question to whomever was standing beside her.

"Doctor Parker."

"Yes."

"They say we'll be coming along in a second car and you can see us for yourself. Just wait for the call, but get Demi and Taylor up and ready to go."

"How many of them are there?"

She didn't reply.

"Mrs. Walker?"

"It's my sister?" Demi cried.

Taylor sat up.

Allan heard the phone go dead. He held the cell phone at his ear nevertheless and tried to think of what he would tell Demi. If he told her all of it too quickly, she would surely panic. He was close to it himself.

"They went to your sister's home," he began.

"Who? Warren, those men?"

"Yes."

"I can't believe him. I didn't think he was stupid enough to go that far. I guess I made another mistake. Damn it. I hope Lois called the police. Did she say if she had?"

Allan stared silently. Even in the darkness, he thought he could see Demi's eyes widen.

"They're still there?"

"Yes."

"Oh, my God."

"What, Mom?" Taylor asked, grinding the sleep out of his eyes.

"They were telling her what to tell me, what to get us to do. They're threatening to hurt them all. I'm sorry. We've got to get dressed," Allan said.

"Where are we going?"

"I don't know. Someone's calling me in about twenty minutes with that information."

"What will we do? Should we call the police? What about Lois, Ralph, and Jodi? Allan!" she cried when he didn't respond.

"I don't know yet, Demi. I've got to think. These are ruthless people."

"Then let's just call the police now. I want Warren arrested."

"You can't arrest him now," Allan said, heading for his clothes. He turned on the lights.

"Why not?"

"He's dead," he said.

"Dead? Warren's dead?"

"Yes."

"But . . . how did he die?"

Allan paused to look at her but didn't answer.

"They killed him?"

"Yes."

"Why? Why would they kill Warren? He's the one who brought Taylor to that man's home. I don't understand."

"Obviously, he disappointed them, and they felt he was no longer needed," Allan explained.

"Disappointed them? My God."

"That's why I'm saying we've got to be careful, Demi, think this out carefully. I don't want any more harm coming to any of your family."

Demi didn't speak. She nodded, the terror now chilling her body. She looked at Taylor.

He shrugged.

"I tried to tell you Warren's elevator never got to the top floor, Mom."

"This is no time for jokes, Taylor."

"I know. But I'd rather be funny than scared."

"Oh, Taylor." She started to cry. He put his hand on her shoulder and then hugged her.

"I'll be all right, "she promised.

"Sure. We'll all be all right." He looked at Allan but didn't see the same confidence in his face. "Mom, let's just give them what they want and go home," he told her, and went to get his clothes on quickly, too.

Demi looked at Allan. She could read it in his eyes.

He wished it were just that easy now.

CHAPTER TWELVE

Scooter made the next call to Allan himself.

"Doctor Parker, I presume," he said when Allan answered. "Give me your exact location."

He listened and then played with his PDA for a few moments. Ralph, Lois, and Jodi sat on the sofa, Jodi on Lois's lap and Ralph as closely to them as he could. They watched and listened to Scooter as he spoke.

Frankie was asleep in the easy chair, and Tony was still eating cookies and drinking coffee in the kitchen doorway.

"Okay, Doctor Parker, I have your directions to the location for you."

He rattled it off.

"I want you to call me when you reach this intersection," he said and described it. "Here's the number you will call: 555-434-5044."

He hung up and stood.

"Time to get the show on the road," he said. He nodded at Frankie and Tony moved quickly to wake him. "Let's go, Walker family," he ordered.

Ralph and Lois stood up, Lois still clinging to Jodi.

"Wait a minute," Ralph said. He looked down at Warren's corpse, now covered with a blanket. "What about him?"

"What about him? You want me to put him in the trunk?" Scooter asked. Tony laughed.

"No, but . . . how are we supposed to explain that afterward?" Ralph asked and narrowed his eyes. "You won't let us go no matter what you get from my nephew. How could you with a dead body in our home to explain?"

Scooter shook his head and muttered, "Ralph, Ralph, Ralph. We're not exactly amateurs here. I was about to tell you to leave the door unlocked. There are people coming by to take care of that," Scooter said, nodding at Warren's body as if it were just so much refuse now. "They are good at what they do. It will all be cleaned up and so well that you would have a hard time convincing the police anything happened here whatsoever. Does that answer your question?"

"I guess," Ralph said.

"Unless, of course, you'd prefer that we leave him."

"Of course not."

"All right then. You won't have a body. You will come home to your house the way it was before we arrived and that's it. You can all go on with your happy, little lives. We'll be out of your lives, unless you insist on keeping us. Do I make myself clear?" Scooter asked.

Ralph looked at Lois, who was probably hanging on a thread as it was. He nodded and went to the front door to unlock it.

Frankie stood and washed his face with his dry palms. He looked very tired, very weak.

"You all right, Frankie?" Scooter asked.

"Yeah, sure. I'm fine."

"Good, because Ralph here is very concerned about everyone, even the dead."

"I just wanted to know what I had to anticipate afterward. That's all," Ralph said in an apologetic tone when he turned back.

"I understand. No problem." Scooter started to move and then stopped to look at Ralph again. "What do you do for a living, Ralph?"

"I'm an accountant, CPA."

"Oh. Well that explains why you like everything in tidy little places. Shall we dance?" Scooter asked. "You three and I will ride in your car, Ralph. Tony and Mr. Vico will follow right behind us. You'll drive, Ralph. You think you're up to it?"

Ralph said nothing and then nodded.

"The garage door is through the kitchen," he muttered. Lois lifted Jodi to carry her.

"She's a big girl. She can walk," Scooter told her.

"She's very frightened."

"That's because you're telegraphing your fear," Scooter said, suddenly behaving like some sort of a psychologist. "Get hold of yourself. It will go easier on your daughter." He didn't move.

Ralph's eyes widened. How could it possibly matter whether his wife carried his daughter or not? he wondered. He looked at Lois and shook his head, doing the best he could to warn her that they weren't dealing with a stable person. He was a cold psychopath. He could kill one of them as coolly as he had killed Warren.

Lois understood and lowered Jodi to the floor. She took her hand and looked quickly at Scooter to see if he would complain about that, too.

Scooter smiled and brushed the top of Jodi's head.

"You want to be a big girl now, don't you? You don't want your mother carrying you around."

Jodi looked up at Lois, who tried to give the best reassuring smile she could.

Scooter nodded at Ralph, and they all marched out to the garage. Ralph opened the door, and Scooter opened the rear car door.

"I'll sit with Jodi," he said, taking her other hand. "You go up front with your husband, Lois."

"No."

"No? Would you rather I left you here with Mr. Moore? You and he can discuss it, even though it will be a one-sided conversation."

"Please. She's terrified," Lois said.

"No, she's not." Scooter laughed. "She's too tired to be afraid, right Jodeeeeee?" he said.

Jodi looked at her mother and then at Scooter. He reached down and lifted her into the rear seat.

"Get in the front," he ordered Lois. "Now. We're not wasting another second here."

She bit down on her lower lip to keep herself from screaming and went around to the passenger's front door.

Ralph got in and she followed, turning immediately to smile and comfort Jodi, who sat obediently.

"You'll be all right, honey. Mommy's right here."

Scooter nodded at Tony.

"You stay close. You have the general directions in case we get separated."

"We won't get separated," Tony said. He glanced at Frankie, who was still looking quite peaked and tired. "Ready, boss?"

"Yeah, yeah. Let's get moving," Frankie said, coming back to life.

They walked out to Frankie's car.

"Okay, back out and go right," Scooter ordered Ralph. He did so, closing the garage, and then started away.

"Where are we going?"

"Get us onto the 10 Freeway West. I'll give you directions after that," Scooter said. He smiled at Jodi. "Now, aren't we all cozy. This is going to be fun."

Lois looked back at him. He did seem to be enjoying it all. It was difficult to believe that such men really existed and weren't simply the figments of some movie writer's imagination. There was nothing unreal about this.

"Please turn around and mind your own business now, Lois," he said. "You're making Jodi and me very nervous, and we both hate being nervous, right, Jodeeeeee?"

Lois tried to give her daughter a comforting smile, but it was clear that Jodi was in a daze, too frightened to speak, maybe even blocking out what she saw and heard. Lois glanced at Scooter and then turned around just as

Ralph lowered his right hand to find her left hand. She seized his, and they squeezed each other's palm gently, reassuringly.

"We'll be all right," he whispered. "I promise."

"Don't drive too fast, Ralph," Scooter warned. "We don't want to lose Tony, and if a policeman comes after us, there'll be a lot of misery."

Ralph eased off the accelerator.

Nearly forty minutes later, Scooter's cell phone rang. It had *Twinkle Twinkle Little Star* as a ring tone.

Scooter opened his cell phone.

"Have you reached the intersection I described?" Scooter asked Allan. "Good. Follow Beacon Road to Sunset Street and make a right turn. As any GPS will tell you, your destination is on the right. We're not far behind. See you soon, Doctor," he added and closed his phone.

He looked at Jodi who had perked up at the ring tone. "You like that?"

He played it again for her. She didn't smile. She couldn't smile no matter what Scooter did for her. The blood-splattered face of the man she had begun to call Uncle Warren remained glued to her inner eyes. Scooter wasn't pleased.

"You know," he said, leaning toward her, "you're a lucky little girl. You could have been food for worms by now as I understand it. You should be more grateful, more appreciative."

"You're frightening her. Leave her alone!" Lois cried.

Scooter glared at her and then smiled.

"Of course. Very soon, we'll be leaving you all alone," he said.

The words should have been promising, but they didn't help Lois to relax and feel better. They made her feel worse.

"It's a veterinarian clinic," Demi announced the moment it came into view. "I don't understand."

"What's the problem, Mom?" Taylor asked. He leaned forward. "They're all a bunch of animals. This is logical."

Despite his own trepidation, Allan couldn't help but laugh.

"Maybe he's right. Actually, it's no surprise to me. They couldn't just waltz into some hospital, clinic, or whatever with all of us and get what they want. They must have some connection, some way to work this place into their objectives. It's somewhat primitive considering what I might have to do, but for what they want, what they think will help Mr. Vico, this place should suffice. I'm sure the necessary medical equipment will be in there."

"Exactly who are these people, Allan?"

He shook his head. "I don't know for certain, Demi, but the man I'm speaking with now is different from the men Taylor and I confronted. There's a cold confidence in his voice. He has a more professional air about him, if there is such a thing for these kinds of men."

"You're confident the necessary equipment is in there?" Demi asked, now more motivated to end this.

"We don't need very sophisticated stuff. Antiseptic material, hypodermics, tubes, bandages. What won't be in there is what they'll need if what I think can happen, happens."

"What does that mean?" she asked, her heart pounding again. "What can happen?"

His phone rang.

"Doctor Parker. Yes, we're pulling into the parking lot now. Okay," he said and closed his cell. "They want us to wait in the car."

Demi looked at the animal clinic. It was located on a secondary street in a fairly wooded area. The nearest house was at least a quarter of a mile away. The building itself was a long, single story, light-pink stucco structure. They could hear dogs barking in the rear. There was only one window lit, but the clinic had good outside lighting.

"Did they say anything more about Lois, Ralph, and Jodi?" Demi asked.

"No."

"How do we know they are really with them? Maybe they already . . ."

"Don't do this to yourself, Demi," he urged.

She shook her head. "It looks so deserted here. We're so helpless."

"There must be someone who stays with the animals overnight," Allan said.

"What exactly do they expect you to do, Allan?"

"Extract some blood from Taylor and inject it into Mr. Vico," he said. "It won't take long, and what we want to do is get out of there as soon as I've done it because—"

"Because what?"

"As I was about to say, it's a crapshoot when it comes

to this sort of thing. I don't have Vico's medical records. I don't know his blood type. Taylor as an O/Rh negative is as close as you can be to a universal donor, but the antibodies could very likely cause a fatal reaction. Vico could suffer a hemolytic transfusion reaction."

"What exactly does that mean?"

"People who get the wrong blood type get real sick, Mom," Taylor said.

"Let Doctor Parker explain it, Taylor."

"We all have these little markers called antigens on the surface of our red blood cells. There are two very important systems of antigens that have to be matched before anyone can get a transfusion. The body attacks the wrong ones if they're transfused because it sees it as a foreign substance, and that defense can be fatal. Organs can shut down, people can get cardiac arrest."

"A heart attack," Taylor said, gleefully. Demi looked at him and then at Allan.

"Yes, that's possible."

"How fast will you know if that's going to happen, Allan?"

"Pretty fast. He would get fever, chills, become nauseous. I don't know how sophisticated these bad guys are, but if they're not, I can snow them under long enough for us to get out, assuming they uphold their side of the bargain.

"The complication here," he continued, "is Vico's had two full doses of chemotherapy and is already in a somewhat weakened, precarious state."

"Poor guy," Taylor said.

"I wouldn't be flippant about this, Taylor. They killed Warren," Demi reminded him.

Taylor was about to make another sarcastic comment when they saw headlights on the dark street behind them. Demi seized Allan's arm.

"Easy," he said.

"They could kill us all."

"I don't think so. That would be quite a mess to cover up," Allan told her. He didn't want to admit it, but it was more like a prayer.

They watched the two vehicles turn into the driveway. Demi leaned to her right to see Lois and Ralph.

"Ralph's driving the second car," she said happily. "I see Lois. They're all right."

She started to open the door.

"Don't," Allan said, reaching across the seat to grab her arm. "Don't do anything until they tell us to do it. You don't want them to feel threatened in any way."

She closed the door. They watched Scooter step out of Ralph's car. When he opened the door, Demi could see Jodi in the car light. She looked so tiny, as if she had shrunken with fear.

Tony quickly came up beside Scooter and, after a few words, got into Ralph's car's rear seat and closed the door. Frankie Vico made his way slowly to join Scooter. It looked like even those few steps were difficult for him.

"Why don't they let Ralph, Lois, and Jodi out? Why did that man get in with them?" Demi asked.

"They want us to understand they're still hostages," Allan said. "Maybe you should stay in the car, too, Demi."

"No. I won't let Taylor in there without me."

"Then keep your cool. Just take it easy. You don't want to spook them. We'll get out of this. I promise," he said.

Scooter approached their car, and Allan rolled down his window.

"We'll go inside now, Doc, and you'll do your magic. You do it well, the boy and his mother get into your car and Ralph and his family can drive off with you. Understand?"

Allan nodded. "Are you sure everything I need is in there?"

"Everything you wanted and more has all been arranged, yes. There's an animal caretaker here, but he's been instructed to remain in the back. Let's go."

Allan, Demi, and Taylor got out. Frankie Vico glared at Allan.

"You brought this on yourself, Doc. You and Doctor Weber playing God. Well, now I'm playing God," he said.

"And I'm the Angel of Death," Scooter added. "Or maybe just an angel. Isn't this fun?"

He nodded at the front entrance. Allan put his arm around Taylor, who held Demi's hand. The three of them walked to the animal clinic. Demi looked back at Lois and Ralph, but it was difficult to see because of the shadows draping the automobile.

There was a small lobby dimly lit by the light spilling from the open door of the room just behind it. Scooter led the way, and Frankie followed. Allan noted how weak and tired he looked and behaved. Scooter opened the door to a fairly good size examination room and stepped back for everyone to enter. The moment they did, Allan was surprised at what he saw.

The table had been set up for Frankie, but another table had been set up beside it with a catheter and a plastic bag for collection. The assorted needles, bandages and medications were on a table beside it.

"What's this?" Allan asked. "I explained on the phone that I would need only to use a hypodermic needle the same way a lab technician takes blood for tests. I then inject Mr. Vico. I don't need that much blood, and it would take hours for the transfusion."

"That donation isn't for Mr. Vico. It's for his cousin's daughter-in-law," Scooter said. "It's mainly why I'm here, even though we all love Frankie and want to see him recuperate quickly," he added, smiling at Frankie.

"What's wrong with her?"

"She has breast cancer. So you can help her, too, and be a bigger hero."

"You don't understand. Even . . ."

"It's too late for discussions, Doctor Parker," Scooter said. "I'm not very good at negotiations anyway. I don't have the patience. We take care of Frankie and then junior contributes a pint for another purpose."

Allan looked at Demi and then at Taylor, who he could see had finally lost his bravado.

"That wasn't part of our bargain."

"Hey, you're not exactly in a position to bargain, Doc," Scooter said.

"Listen to me, please," Allan pleaded. "The results we've had with this . . . I can't even call it experimental procedure . . . it was first a pure accident, and then I went ahead and . . ."

"Oh, Doc, please. You're wasting everyone's time, and Frankie here will be the first to tell you that there is no time to waste," Scooter said. He took out his pistol. "Look, there is someone here who is not necessary for our purposes," he added, looking at Demi. "Shall I convince you of our determination the way I used Warren to convince Mr. and Mrs. Walker?"

"No," Allan said quickly. "All right, all right. Let's get Mr. Vico comfortable."

"You get him comfortable," Scooter ordered.

Allan helped Frankie take off his jacket. He could see from his complexion and his eyes that he was near exhaustion. His breathing wasn't regular, and he surely had an elevated blood pressure. He helped him lay down on the table and fixed the pillow under his head. Then he rolled up the sleeve of his left arm and nodded at Taylor.

Taylor sauntered over to his table, brushed it off, and then hopped up on it.

"Haircut and shave, please," he said.

Scooter laughed. "Cool kid," he said. "Smart."

"I just want to help Mr. Vico get along," Taylor said, his bravado returning.

Demi took a deep breath and stepped back so she could shake her head at Taylor without Scooter seeing.

Taylor laid back. Allan prepared Taylor's arm, unwrapped the syringe, and found the vein.

"How much you taking for Frankie?" Scooter asked.

Allan looked at Taylor.

"Twenty-four cc's," he replied and began filling the tubes. As soon as he had four, he began to transfer the blood to another hypodermic.

"Why don't you start the kid on the pint?" Scooter suggested, waving his pistol at the catheter.

"Let me do this right, first, please. I don't want to waste anything or make any errors."

Scooter smiled at Demi. "It's great to have a concerned, professional physician with us, isn't it?"

She backed up another step and looked at the door. The building, except for the muffled sound of the dogs now barking more intently, was quiet and dark.

Allan approached Frankie. He had his eyes closed and then opened them slightly.

"You all right?" Allan asked him.

"Get on with it," Frankie ordered. "I seen what you did for that guy. Do it for me."

"Look, the circumstances weren't exactly similar. I know to a layman it looks . . ."

"I don't want to hear your medical bullshit. I'm dying anyway, ain't I?"

"We're all dying," Scooter said, glaring at Allan. "Some faster than others, faster than they ever imagined."

"All right," Allan said. "I'll do what you ask," he said and began injecting the blood. He watched Frankie's eyes and his breathing carefully. After the second tube, he saw Frankie shudder.

"Damn cold in here, ain't it?" he said.

"Not as cold as the grave," Scooter offered. Frankie grunted.

Allan injected another tube.

"I don't feel so good. You sure you're doing this right?"

"You're still suffering the side effects of your chemother-apy, Mr. Vico," Allan said. He glanced at Scooter, who shrugged and smirked.

He really couldn't care less about Frankie, Allan real-ized. Someone far more powerful is running this show.

After the next tube was injected, Frankie squirmed.

"I think . . . I'm going to throw up," he said.

"If you do, heave the other way," Scooter said. "This normal?" he asked Allan.

"People have a variety of reactions to transfusions, yes."

Frankie's complexion whitened more. He groaned and then brought his hands to his chest.

"I don't feel so good," he said.

"Doc?" Scooter asked.

"Give it time. Relax, Mr. Vico."

"Get started on the kid," Scooter ordered.

Frankie moaned.

"I don't like this," he said. "Something's not right."

"Let me get him a glass of water," Allan said turning.

"Forget him. He got his, now get to the kid," Scooter ordered firmly.

Allan glanced at Demi. She looked petrified. Frankie squirmed more, moaned louder, complained of being too hot, then too cold.

"Shut the fuck up," Scooter told him. "Let's go," he told Allan and waved his pistol.

Allan moved back to Taylor. Frankie struggled to sit up.

"Hey, relax," Scooter told him.

"I don't like it. It's worse than the fucking chemo . . . somethin' . . . he poisoned me or somethin' . . ."

"With blood? Don't be an idiot. I'm standing here watching him," Scooter said.

Frankie shook his head, rubbed his kidney, and then started to dry heave.

Scooter leaped backward to avoid getting sprayed if he started throwing up.

"What the hell is this?" he asked Allan. "It don't seem normal to me."

"I think he's having a hemolytic transfusion reaction," Allan said. "I tried to tell you, but . . ."

Frankie swung himself off the table. He wobbled.

"What the hell's a hemo whatever?"

"It can be serious. This looks like it is. He's going to need to go to an emergency room immediately," Allan said.

"Emergency room? This is the emergency room, and you've got one helluva emergency on your hands if you don't get moving on that kid," Scooter said. He eyed Frankie who wobbled again, grasping the table to keep himself from toppling.

"Forget the kid," Frankie muttered. "Get me to the hospital. You heard him. Something's gone wrong."

"Get you to . . . what are you fucking out of your mind?" Scooter said. "You're going to die anyway, ain'tcha? Just lay down."

Frankie looked at Allan.

"You did this . . . you . . . Tony!" he screamed.

"Shut the fuck up," Scooter said. He stepped toward him.

Frankie shook his head.

"Tony will get me to the hospital," he said.

"You're fucking this up," Scooter said. "He can't leave those people and take you to the hospital."

"I'm going," Frankie insisted and started toward the door.

Scooter seized him at the back of his neck and shoved him back toward the table. He hit it and spun toward Scooter, who put his hand on his chest to hold him back. Desperate and in total panic, Frankie reached down, grabbed the emptied syringe and shoved it into Scooter's chest, right at his heart. Scooter, shocked, looked down at the needle dangling there.

"What the fuck . . ."

He swung his pistol and caught Frankie on the left temple. He struggled to hold on, but Scooter hit him again, and he fell back against the table and then slowly sat, stunned.

Demi screamed. Scooter started to turn toward her, but Allan charged forward and grabbed Scooter's arm with his left hand while pushing hard on the syringe still in Scooter's chest. They struggled, doing what looked like a strange Kabuki dance because Scooter's strength seemed to be seeping out of his body through the syringe along with the blood that was now leaking faster around the needle. He wore a look of total surprise as Allan got the upper hand and managed to shake the pistol from his grip. The moment it fell, Demi seized it.

And then suddenly, Scooter stopped struggling. It looked like he was smiling.

His legs buckled, and his tall, lean body poured downward to crumble at Allan's feet.

For a long moment, no one moved.

"Wow. Good work, Doc," Taylor said.

Allan kneeled beside Frankie Vico. His eyes were still opened, but he was in a daze, his breathing heavy and difficult. He gasped.

"He's going into cardiac arrest," Allan said.

Demi turned toward the window.

"Lois, Ralph, and Jodi," she cried in a whisper.

CHAPTER THIRTEEN

"How long are we supposed to sit out here?" Ralph asked. He wasn't as timid about confronting Tony as he had been confronting Scooter.

"Long as it takes," Tony said.

"I'd like to take my daughter to the bathroom."

Tony looked at Jodi, who had pressed herself tightly to the corner of the seat in order to keep herself as far as possible from him.

"She ain't complaining."

"She's too frightened to complain."

"I'd like to take a piss, too. She'll hold it in. Put a cork in it," he told Jodi and laughed.

"How can you do this?" Lois asked him. He stared at her as if the question had been asked in a foreign language. "How can you be so cruel to a child?"

"You talk too much," he replied instead of answering. "If I was you, I'd shut my mouth."

They all turned when Demi stepped out of the front entrance of the clinic.

"What the hell is she doing out here? Don't nobody do nothin' until I say," Tony ordered. He opened his door as

Demi started toward them. "Hey, where's Frankie? What's going on?"

"Doctor Parker says we've got to get him to the nearest hospital emergency room," she replied, continuing toward them. "It didn't go well in there. Doctor Parker says Mr. Vico's having a hemolytic transfusion reaction. He needs your help immediately."

"Hemo, what?"

"A bad reaction to the blood transfusion," she said.

"That's bullshit."

"No, it's not bullshit," she countered firmly. "Mr. Vico sent me out here to get you to help him. Doctor Parker can't leave him. You have to hurry," she said.

"Where's Scooter? Why can't he help him? Why can't Doctor Parker?"

"The man you call Scooter and Mr. Vico had an argument, and Scooter is dead."

Tony just smiled.

"Dead? How's he dead?"

"Mr. Vico had a fight with him and killed him," Demi said "You can see it all for yourself."

"Why would they fight?"

"Scooter wasn't very concerned about your friend. He didn't care if he had a bad reaction or not," she explained. "Well?" she followed when he didn't move.

"Frankie killed him? How could he kill anyone? He's half dead himself. This is just a bunch crap. You'd better tell me the truth and fast," Tony said, pointing the pistol at her.

"I am telling you the truth. When you go in, you will see for yourself," Demi said. "If I were you, I'd hurry. Doctor Parker thinks Mr. Vico could die any minute. He said he's going into cardiac arrest and he needs to get him on a defibrillator."

"De . . . what?"

"You're wasting precious time. He's dying!" Demi cried, her arms out.

Tony stopped smiling. He pulled back the hammer on his .38 and pointed at her.

"If you're lying, you're all dead meat."

"I'm not lying," Demi said firmly. "Would Mr. Vico or your Scooter permit me to come walking out here like this to lie to you?"

Tony thought a moment. That did make sense.

"All right. Everyone out. Now!" he screamed.

Lois moved quickly to get out and open the rear door for Jodi. She embraced her quickly. Ralph stepped out, and Tony followed, stepping back so he was a safe distance from both Demi and Ralph.

"What happened, Demi?" Ralph asked.

"Just what I said. Mr. Vico had a reaction to the transfusion. He was stubborn and wouldn't listen to Doctor Parker. He tried to explain that blood type plays a critical role in all this," she explained loudly enough for Tony to hear it all.

She looked back at Tony, hoping he followed the explanation and wouldn't do anything impulsive. He looked like he was starting to believe her.

"When he asked to go to the hospital, the man called Scooter wouldn't let him, so they got into a fight," she added.

"You're absolutely sure Scooter is dead?" Tony asked, his face clouded with confusion and incredulity.

"You'll see it all for yourself, but please, for Mr. Vico's sake, move quickly."

"All right. You all go ahead of me," Tony said, waving the pistol at them.

Lois, now carrying Jodi, came around and joined Demi and Ralph, who started for the animal clinic's front entrance.

"Is Taylor all right?" Lois asked.

"Yes."

"And Doctor Parker?"

"He's okay," Demi said. "As soon as we enter and the lights go on, move to your left and kneel," she whispered. "Nothing more," she emphasized. "We'll all be all right soon. I promise."

"What?"

"Quit talking so much," Tony ordered.

Demi moved faster and opened the front door. She stepped back to let Ralph, Lois, and Jodi enter. Tony gestured for her to enter, too.

Demi stepped in, and Tony followed. Just as he entered the lobby, Taylor, hovering on the left, turned on the lights. Before Tony could respond, Allan pushed the office chair on which Scooter's corpse was tied with some adhesive bandage. It rolled toward Tony, whose eyes bulged with surprise. The hypodermic was still lodged in Scooter's chest.

"Drop your gun now," Allan said, holding Scooter's pistol pointed at him.

Confused for a moment, Tony hesitated and then brought up his pistol toward Allan, who fired first. Tony's chest seemed to open like a bloodred rose, and he fell back. No one moved. He moaned, and then, he expired, his fingers releasing the pistol. There was a long moment of total silence as the echo of the gun died away.

Jodi started to cry softly. Lois embraced her.

"Where's Frankie Vico?" Ralph asked, looking down at Tony.

"In the examination room," Allan said. "He went into cardiac arrest. There wasn't much I could do."

Ralph smiled.

"You were telling the truth," he said to Demi, who could barely nod. Taylor came to her side, and she put her arm around his shoulders.

Allan looked from Scooter to Tony.

"There goes my Hippocratic oath not to do deliberate harm to anyone."

His weak attempt to lighten the moment fell flat. Lois sat on the small lobby sofa and, still holding Jodi, started to cry. Ralph moved quickly to them. Demi, still shaking herself, tried to smile.

"My God, we're all unharmed."

"Yes, but what do we do now?" Ralph asked.

"I don't know about anyone else," Taylor said, "but I'm ready for breakfast."

That did bring smiles to everyone but Allan. Demi stepped toward him.

"Allan, what do we do now?" she asked.

"Here's the situation," he said. "We call the police and there will be an investigation, of course. It will come out that they were after Taylor's blood, and it could all begin again."

"What choice do we have?" Ralph asked. "There are three dead men here. We were kidnapped, and we all barely escaped with our lives. I never believed that man," he said nodding at Scooter, whose opened eyes and mouth gave the eerie impression that he was reacting to all that had just happened. "I never believed they would simply let us all go, especially after the cold way he killed Warren."

"I understand." Allan hesitated, looked at Demi, and then said, "I suggest we all just get into our cars and drive away. The only other person who knows about the potential in Taylor's white blood cells is Doctor Weber."

"What about the man who sent this guy?" Ralph asked nodding at Scooter. "What about Warren? His body could still be in my home. And even if it isn't, how do we explain his disappearance?"

"Ralph's right," Demi said. She smiled at Allan. "I know you're suggesting this so Taylor is protected, but too much has happened. Even if we could just drive off, and even if we didn't have to worry about what happened to Warren, I'd be worrying all the time about Taylor."

She looked at Taylor. "I wouldn't let him go anywhere himself. He'd soon hate me."

"I wouldn't hate you," Taylor quickly said. "I'd just run away from home. See the world. Maybe join the navy."

"There is no running away from this," Demi said softly. "I realize that now. You know I'm right, Allan."

He nodded. "I'm sorry," he said. He thought he might be saying that for years.

"I have an idea," Taylor interjected.

"What? Find a way to go to Mars?" Allan asked.

"No, not exactly. But . . . what if I'm a fake?"

"What? A fake?"

"What if Jodi's standard treatment at the hospital is what saved her? You said the other patient still doesn't know what you did for him. Because you were testing my blood, Mr. Vico, who found out, did what he did. He was just a desperate guy, and Warren . . ." He looked at his mother. "Warren was nothing more than a money-grubbing guy who got himself in too deeply. They killed him because he made promises that couldn't be fulfilled. In fact, this whole thing happened because you couldn't save Mr. Vico with my blood and Mr. Scooter was upset with him. The rest happened just like it happened."

No one spoke. Allan stared at Taylor and then he smiled.

"Who is this masked man?"

"A cloud of dust and a hearty 'Hi Ho, Silver,'" Taylor said.

"Okay. We'll try it. Except for Joe Weber and myself and you people, no one else knows Taylor's no fake."

"I'm for it," Ralph said. Lois nodded.

"Demi?" Allan asked.

"Okay, but I'll still worry."

"You're supposed to, Mom," Taylor said. "It comes with motherhood."

"Don't get a swelled head, Taylor. You're still my little boy."

Allan laughed, and then he flipped open his cell phone and called 911.

As it turned out, it was a good thing that Warren's body was still at the Walker's house. It helped support the idea that Warren had promised too much to the wrong people and that his attempt to make money off such a possibility led to his death. Allan's testimony was that as a research scientist, he was interested in any possibilities, but the results of further testing and examination revealed it was a dead end. He had gotten to Joe first, and they agreed that would be their story. Joe Weber would have agreed to almost anything after he had heard what Allan and the others had endured.

During the interrogation, Allan was good at performing his great disappointment. He even referred to the experiments with the cancer-resistant mice and got into a detailed discussion of the innate immune system, delineating the properties of leukocytes, monocytes, and the NK cell. The investigating detective, Frankie Randall, a stout 50-year-old dreaming of retirement, nearly fell asleep during Allan's lecture.

"So you see," he concluded, "why I needed to be here, but I never imagined anything like this."

"Yeah, none of us do," Randall said. "You ever use a thirty-eight before, Doc?"

"Thirty-eight?"

"The pistol you used to shoot Tony Marino?"

"Oh. Yes. I mean, no, never."

"I guess you were just lucky."

"Well, I knew how to pull a trigger, and he was close enough," Allan said.

"I've seen many an amateur miss at that range. All right. Thanks," Randall said. "We'll be in touch."

Allan thanked him and left the examination room. Demi was waiting for him in the police station lobby. Taylor had gone home with Ralph, Lois, and Jodi. Everyone was both physically and emotionally exhausted.

"You're not starting back to Los Angeles now, are you?" Demi asked him.

"I was thinking of that, yes."

"Spend another day and night," she suggested. "You don't realize how tired you are, Allan. It will all hit you like a sledgehammer soon."

"Now who's playing doctor?" he replied, smiling.

"I can play doctor," she teased.

He went home with her. Taylor was staying with Lois and Ralph so they had the house to themselves. The first thing he did was take a shower. He wasn't in the shower stall a minute before the door opened and she, naked, stepped in beside him.

"Mind?" she asked.

"I'd be out of my mind if I did," he said, and they kissed.

They made what he thought was wonderful love right afterward. Both of them having been so close to death, they needed to reinforce their sense of life, but the attraction to each other that they had begun to feel suddenly blossomed, or, as Allan would say later, exploded.

"It felt like fireworks to me," she said.

The lovemaking stirred up both of their appetites, and she prepared a delicious pasta and clam sauce. They opened wine and talked incessantly, neither willing to let a moment of silence exist between them.

Afterward, they went upstairs to sleep, but both lay awake for a long time, still reliving some of the terror.

"Tomorrow, I'll pack up everything that was Warren's and get it out of the house," she said.

"You want me to hang around to help?"

"I'd like you to hang around, but not for that. Believe me, it's not going to take me long."

He laughed, and they kissed and embraced. They started to fall asleep in each other's arms and parted. Neither woke up before Taylor came home. Allan was the first to sense him standing in the doorway.

"What's wrong?" Demi asked, seeing him sit up quickly. He nodded at the doorway.

"Oh. Hi, Taylor."

"Hi, Mom," Taylor replied. "Does this mean we get free medical care from now on?"

"You think I'm that cheap?" Demi responded. She even surprised herself.

Taylor's eyebrows went up. When he smiled, she thought she was surely looking at Buddy. Maybe I am. Maybe he's showing me his approval.

"Don't mind me," he said. "My morals were corrupted years ago."

They both laughed and fell back to their pillows.

Later, Allan stopped to see Joe before he headed back to Los Angeles. They talked for a while about what they should do next.

"It's not so easy anymore, Joe. Things have become a little complicated for me," Allan said.

Joe smiled.

"Does this mean the great Allan Parker is not a medical robot after all?"

"I'm not sure if that's good or bad, but it's true," he confessed. "You'll probably see a lot more of me in the near future."

They left it at that, and Allan returned to his work in Los Angeles. He spent almost every weekend for the next five months in Palm Springs, and twice Demi came to be with him in L.A. One night, as they were returning to her home after dinner, she just continued to sit in the car when they had pulled into the driveway and he had turned off the engine.

"Something wrong?" Allan asked.

"No, not wrong," she said. "But there is something."

He sat back.

"I'm all ears," he said.

"I don't know if it's fair to say it or not, but I'm never fully relaxed with you, Allan."

"Oh?"

"It's not your fault," she said quickly. She turned to him. "I keep waiting for you to ask."

"You to marry me?"

"No," she said laughing, "although, that wouldn't be a bad question. No," she added, returning to her serious expression, "I keep expecting you to ask for Taylor's blood."

"I have been afraid to do that," he admitted. "Not because I fear that you'll say no, but that you'd think that was the main reason I'm seeing you. I wouldn't blame you for thinking that. I know what I was like, what I am like, to a certain extent."

"Why do I feel guilty hearing that?" she asked.

"Probably for the same reason I feel guilty for not asking you. I've suddenly put my personal interests and pleasures before my life's work. I feel terribly selfish, but when I am confronted with the choice of going on with the research and possibly losing you, I chose not to lose you."

"So then are you going to ask me?"

"For Taylor's blood?"

"No, silly, your first thought."

"Oh. Oh yeah."

"When exactly are you or do you expect you will get around to doing that?"

"You know, I can see where Taylor gets his wiseass," Allan said.

She laughed.

"Demi Petersen, will you marry me?"

"Are you asking just to get free haircuts? That's what Taylor's going to want to know."

"Yes. I expect that, among two or three million other things," Allan said.

She leaned toward him, and they kissed.

As it turned out, he never asked her to have Taylor donate his blood samples for the research. It happened a different way. He had come into Palm Springs early on a Friday a month after their engagement, and Demi had asked him to pick up Taylor at school. She was still nervous about it all, despite the way the story had faded.

"Hey," Allan said when Taylor came sauntering out of the school, his head down as usual. "How do you know where you're walking?"

"ESP," Taylor said. He looked out at his classmates getting into cars and onto buses. "When we move to L.A., she's going to have to loosen the chains," he muttered.

"Don't worry, she will," Allan said pulling away.

"I've come up with a wedding gift for you guys," Taylor said.

"Oh?"

"A pint of my blood," Taylor said.

Allan slowed down.

"Did you tell your mother that?"

"Nope. It's a surprise."

"Are you sure? She's going to be . . ."

"Nervous and frightened at first, but I'm sure you'll work out a way that keeps it surreptitious. I love that word."

Allan laughed. "What made you decide to do it, Taylor?"

"Bobby Pearson's mother has breast cancer. He's in my class. He looks like he was visited by a vampire. It's what happened to your mother, too, right?"

"Yes," Allan said.

"Well, Doc, it's time we put a bullet in that monster's heart," Taylor said.

Allan didn't reply. He fought back the tears that were demanding to fall.

"But don't be fooled, Doc," Taylor continued. "I still firmly believe you love my mother."

"I do, Taylor."

"But only because you're getting free haircuts," he said.

Allan laughed. He laughed longer and harder than he could remember, and that laughter disguised his tears.

Yes, he thought, we'll put a bullet in that monster's heart. One day soon, we will.

They drove on, one carrying the magic in his young body, and the other dreaming of becoming a magician.

WILLIAM S. SCHAILL

A NUCLEAR TIMEBOMB

A sunken Soviet nuclear sub lies silently off the coast of Puerto Rico, three hundred meters below the surface. But its experimental plutonium reactor has become unstable, leaking radiation into the sea—radiation that endangers not only Puerto Rico, but America's entire Eastern seaboard.

A DEADLY PRIZE

The Russian government secretly turns to famed U.S. salvage expert Al Madeira to quietly retrieve their deadly cargo, but as Madeira sets to work he quickly realizes he's not the only interested party. Soon he's caught in a vise between the U.S. government, the Russian government, and the Russian mob, with global security hanging in the balance.

SEAGLOW

ISBN 13: 978-0-8439-4429-7

RISK FACTOR

"A gripping psychological thriller."
— *Publishers Weekly*

When they found the nurse she was already dead. Sitting next to her body, covered in blood and holding a knife, was seventeen-year-old Garret, a patient in the psychiatric ward of the hospital. Dr. Molly Katz can't believe it. She's Garret's doctor and she never thought he was capable of anything like this. But now a second nurse has been butchered. Who's stalking the hospital corridors for prey? Could it be Garret after all? As Molly fights to save Garret from the law and his own mind, the eyes of the killer have turned toward her... and her children.

"Compelling...fast-paced."
—*School Library Journal*

Charles Atkins

ISBN 13: 978-0-8439-6085-3

R. Karl Largent

THE MISSION

At the bottom of the Sargasso Sea lies a sunken German U-Boat filled with Nazi gold. For more than half a century the treasure has been waiting—tempting, luring, but always out of reach. Now, Elliott Wages has been hired to join a salvage mission to retrieve the gold, but it isn't long at all before he realizes that there's quite a bit he hasn't been told—and that not everyone wants the mission to succeed.

THE DANGER

The impenetrable darkness of the Sargasso hides more than the submarine's priceless cargo. It hides secret agendas, unrevealed motives, and unbelievable dangers—some natural, others decidedly manmade. But before this mission is over, Elliott Wages will learn firsthand all the deadly secrets cloaked in the inky blackness of...

THE SEA

ISBN 13: 978-0-8439-4495-2

THE COFFIN SHIP

The giant supertanker *Prometheus*, the largest ship on Earth, sits at anchor in the Persian Gulf. In her tanks are 250,000 tons of crude oil. Somewhere on board is a crew member determined that she never completes her voyage to Europe. Already, many of the ship's officers have been killed in a mysterious "accident."

The fate of *Prometheus* rests in the hands of Richard Mariner, the tanker's new captain. It is his responsibility to battle human treachery and the dangers of the open sea to bring *Prometheus* to safe harbor. From the Persian Gulf to the storm-tossed Atlantic, Mariner and his crew will struggle against the elements while trying to uncover the elusive—and cunning—enemy in their midst.

PETER TONKIN

ISBN 13: 978-0-8439-6221-5

Against All Enemies

Like most wars, it started small. When the South American country of San Selva began burning Amazon rain forests, Washington applied pressure to appease popular opinion. But pressure led to attack, and attack led to counter-attack, and soon America found itself in a full-fledged war—against an enemy it was not prepared to fight. Now the stakes are raised and the U.S. sends Special Forces and Navy SEALs to try to regain the upper hand. As the fires in the rain forests rage out of control, ground troops prepare to go in. What started as politics will have to end on the battlefield. But is this a war anyone can win? And at what cost?

Maj. James B. Woulfe, USMC

ISBN 13: 978-0-8439-5140-0

SANDRA
RUTTAN

The police get the call: A four-year-old boy has been found beaten to death in the park. And almost as soon as Hart and Tain arrive at the scene, the case takes a strange turn.

They find the victim's brother hiding in the woods nearby. He says he saw the whole thing and claims his older sister is the killer. And she's missing....

When the boy's father is notified that his son is dead, his first response is to hire a high-powered attorney, who seems determined to create every legal roadblock he can for Hart and Tain. The search is on for the missing girl, and the case is about to get even stranger.

THE
FRAILTY
OF FLESH

ISBN 13: 978-0-8439-6075-4

☐ **YES!**

Sign me up for the Leisure Thriller Book Club and send
my FREE BOOKS! If I choose to stay in the club, I will
pay only $8.50* each month, a savings of $7.48!

NAME: _____

ADDRESS: _____

TELEPHONE: _____

EMAIL: _____

☐ I want to pay by credit card.

☐ **VISA** ☐ **MasterCard.** ☐ **DISCOVER**

ACCOUNT #: _____

EXPIRATION DATE: _____

SIGNATURE: _____

Mail this page along with $2.00 shipping and handling to:
Leisure Thriller Book Club
PO Box 6640
Wayne, PA 19087
Or fax (must include credit card information) to:
610-995-9274

You can also sign up online at **www.dorchesterpub.com**.
*Plus $2.00 for shipping. Offer open to residents of the U.S. and Canada only.
Canadian residents please call 1-800-481-9191 for pricing information.
If under 18, a parent or guardian must sign. Terms, prices and conditions subject to
change. Subscription subject to acceptance. Dorchester Publishing reserves the right
to reject any order or cancel any subscription.